THE KNOCKOFF ECLIPSE

THE KNOCKOFF ECLIPSE

by

Melissa Bull

Anvil Press • Canada

Anvil Press Publishers Inc.
P.O. Box 3008, Main Post Office
Vancouver, B.C. V6B 3X5 Canada
www.anvilpress.com

Library and Archives Canada Cataloguing in Publication

Bull, Melissa, 1977-, author
        The knockoff eclipse / Melissa Bull. — First edition.

Short stories.
ISBN 978-1-77214-120-7 (softcover)

        I. Title.

PS8603.U538K66 2018   C813'.6   C2018-901894-1

Printed and bound in Canada
Cover design by Cecil Lu
Author photo by Alex Tran
Interior by HeimatHouse
Represented in Canada by Publishers Group Canada
Distributed by Raincoast Books

The publisher gratefully acknowledges the financial assistance of the Canada Council for the Arts, the Canada Book Fund, and the Province of British Columbia through the B.C. Arts Council and the Book Publishing Tax Credit.

"This is my life now / Utterly jagged by magic / Insert lyricism later"
— *Maggie Nelson*

"All I ever want to know is how people are making it through life. Where do they put their body, hour by hour, and how do they cope inside of it."
— *Miranda July*

For Mélina

Table of Contents

THE SHAKES

Maybe she invented him. Catherine told Marie-Ève at work that her apartment used to be a clinic and that the doctor who ran it haunts the place now. Catherine said she did her research, and that the clinic was open between 1938 and 1956. The doctor died there. OD'd or hung himself or something. Catherine said she hears him pacing at the same spot on her hardwood floors— in the hall right near the dining room every night. She said that maybe he still thinks he's treating people. Marie-Ève said maybe he doesn't know he's dead. Sometimes that happens.

Catherine's boyfriend is completely passed out. He had two joints after dinner. The gutter trickle sound of the water filter and the light rigged to the side of the fish tank keep her from sleeping. She lies on her back, trying not to move. She feels nausea, then the quick nerve touch of a mild epileptic seizure. It flicks like the Ville-Marie strobe.

She gets up to go to the bathroom. The air is cold and dense in the hall. She pads barefoot into the kitchen. Maybe this was the doctor's operating room. Maybe the doctor isn't the only person who died here.

She pours herself a glass of milk and lights a Peter Jackson. Takes a Lamictal. There's dissipation in her brain. Unhooking.

Maybe he did abortions. Catherine told Marie-Ève about hers that evening as they walked together to the Mont-Royal metro station. Her anti-seizure pills would contort a foetus into abnormality, so now she uses an IUD. But before, she kept falling pregnant.

Catherine lights a second cigarette. She's been having pains in her stomach. Last week she went to the doctor. He told her she has a tumour in her uterus with tentacles that reach up into her *tripes* and grope the edges of her oesophagus.

"I don't know what to tell my parents," she'd said to Marie-Ève as they were closing the store. Marie-Ève had always loved the way Catherine used 1940s anglo jargon in French—*c'était ben swell, ça.* Catherine, Marie-Ève thought, was a real Saguenay beauty—her swingy blunt brown bob brushing her beauty-marked shoulders, her almost almond-shaped velvety brown eyes. Marie-Ève hadn't known what to say to Catherine. She hoped they wouldn't cut her.

Catherine puts out her cigarette. She opens her front door, steps outside for some air. She stands on the front stoop of her ground-floor apartment watching traffic lumber along the boulevard. She can't concentrate on the notion of a tumour's appendages winding within her, embracing her from the inside.

RIVIÈRE ROUGE

Eighteen-wheeler trucks veered along the highway that flanked the other side of the tributary. The noise of their motors echolagged over the river where my stepsister Brigitte and her son, Loïc, swam. Loïc squealed theatrically about the algae, really just to hear the sound of his own voice resonating in the open space. He thrashed his limbs to make the water froth.

I wouldn't get in. I was worried about what else, besides the algae, might be contaminating the water. The river was the road's twin—the sick remnants of something living snaking through the bucolic, gaining momentum, dirtying itself up with Montreal commuters. So I stayed on the dock and checked my shoulders for signs of sunburn.

Brigitte popped up from under water and burst out laughing. Long filaments of algae caught on her arm. She roared and waved mock-threateningly at Loïc, who kicked off toward the other side of the dock. He was fast. Brigitte dove under him. Her purple bikini bottom bubbled over the brown water, then disappeared. She materialized again, her goggles all filled up. Her arms tightened around Loïc and she said in French, "Watch out! The submarine's going to sink!" They went down.

When they came back up, Brigitte wrinkled her nose in disgust. "Hey, Valerie, can you smell that thing from here? Is that stink really coming from the tiny little fish Loïc caught last night?"

On our way in from the city the night before we'd stopped at a general store a couple of kilometres from the cottage for fresh blueberries. Loïc saw a bowl full of worms for sale by the beer fridge and went from blasé city kid to some kind of (admittedly adorable) rhyme about little boys. "Please, please, please can I have the worms? I want to fish, *Maman*. Please?" Brigitte bought him a yogourt container of worms for four bucks. As we grilled kabobs on the barbecue, Loïc discovered an old fishing rod under the back porch of the cottage; he hooked one of the curling worms onto the line and cast it out into the river, and, after a shorter amount of time than either of us had imagined he'd need, managed to catch a small silver fish. He hadn't been able to reel it in, though. He was so little, and he'd never fished. The fishing pole was old, a man's size. For these or whatever other reason, the fish got away, or it died and slipped off his line. Loïc didn't seem to mind. He soon forgot about the fish, ditched the fishing pole, and came up for dinner. And we'd also put it out of our minds until this morning's swim. Now the dead fish flopped by the shore, pushed methodically by currents that weaved up and around granite stones. A motorboat whined by and the fish's stink wafted towards us.

Loïc, who was not bothered by the smell, lifted himself out of the water, ran barefoot across the lawn, and went to play with his trucks on the balcony. Brigitte hefted herself up onto the dock. She lay on her stomach on a lime green beach towel and unhooked her bikini top. She looked from the dock to where the fish floated. "I don't think Didier will be too happy to come all the way to the country to find this," she said. "Maybe while I drive into Montreal with Loïc, you could..?"

"Sure, I'll get rid of it for you."

⚭

Later, Loïc and Brigitte pulled T-shirts over their bathing suits and sat on towels in the car to go to Loïc's soccer game in the city. I watched them disappear down the unpaved road. The car's muffler scraped on the gravel driveway. I walked back to the river, grabbing a stick to keep myself from falling along the steep incline. I poked at the foul-smelling fish that shook in the water like a sequined purse. It wouldn't dislodge. Mosquitoes swarmed. They landed on my arms and thighs, biting freely. The double infestation of pong and insects made me frantic. I waved the stick around my head and swore at the fish. A kitten from a neighbouring cottage walked by and tried to play with the fish, but it floated just out of reach, haloed in flies.

⚭

They were late coming back from the city. Didier was already worked up. "That friend of yours! There's always something! That's why I hate going to those birthday parties. People come up and invite you for lunch and they can't even cook! Can you imagine serving pasta without sauce? I have had your friend over before and I served her bœuf bourguignon! Never pasta without sauce!"

"I just want him to relax." Brigitte's words barely hid her frenetic worry. She scanned the house to make sure nothing was

« 15 »

out of order. "He hasn't been sleeping well this year, you know." She said if he could sleep he'd be in a better mood, but apparently neither could be produced. I'd never seen the guy happy except once at a family pool party in Quebec City, shirtless with his mouth on a bong.

Loïc cried. His narrow shoulders slumped in his grass-stained soccer shirt.

"Okay, okay. It's fine now." Brigitte tried to hush him. She feigned excitement. "Who wants corn on the cob for dinner, now?" Then, to me, "Is it ready?"

I sucked down my breath. Showed her the set table.

"What's that horrible smell? *Non, mais c'est quoi cette odeur!* I come all the way from the city to get away from the smell of garbage just to find this!"

"That's the stinky fish, *Papa*," Loïc ventured, eyes laughing a little through his tears. "I caught it with the worms in the fridge."

I laid the paper napkins on the table and sat beside Loïc. Willing myself quiet.

"You didn't even pour me the good wine, *tabarnak*. What the hell is this crap? What the hell is it?" Crickets thrummed outside. A huge yellow moon hovered over the river, caught in the square of the screen window.

"It's that Santa Cristina. Would you like a beer instead?"

"I told you in the car that beer upsets my stomach. Then I can't sleep! All I want is an *apéritif*, or at least a decent wine. How could you forget the Pernod again? If I weren't the one making all the money maybe there would be some consideration for taste around here. Consideration for taste, *putain*. This stuff is cheap." He finished his wine in a gulp.

Brigitte giggled nervously, eyes cast downward. She helped herself to another cob of corn. "Mmm, these taste like August."

"*Putain*," parroted Loïc.

"When I was your age I had no father! I had no running water! *Merde!* And you make fun of me now? Get out! Finish your plate without another word and get out!"

Tears and snot ran down Loïc's face and into his mouth. His brown hands remained immobile, straight lines superimposed over the cylindrical grid of his buttered corn. The tears cleaned stripes down his dirty face.

I pictured Didier's mouth bleeding from a punch to the face. I saw him spitting out a tooth, writhing in pain from a kick to the scrotum. I set my teeth.

Brigitte put her hand on Loïc's muscular leg. "*Allez, allez*, Loïc. It's okay, just do as your father says and have another bite. It's okay. Don't worry." Loïc tried to swallow his food and his tears, but he choked.

"Look at our son, always crying!"

"Why don't you shut the fuck up for once, you fucking asshole?" I pushed back the bench, slammed open the screen door and paced into the yard overlooking the river.

I could hear him shouting from inside. Each word distinct. "Your *christie d'anglo* sister is enraging me. Tell her to get lost. Eating all our food and insulting us!"

Didier stormed out to his hammock in the forest, the worst place for mosquitoes. No one warned him. Loïc sulked out of the cottage next, sitting by himself on the dock, solitary as his father, steeling himself to whatever thoughts he had. After a moment, he looked at me and shouted: "Just go *home*, Valerie!" His little voice reverberated against the water. Lights in the house across the water extinguished. A truck rumbled by and its sound reached us when it had almost passed from sight.

Brigitte came to me and put a hand on my shoulder. "I guess you'd better leave, Valerie," she said. "I just checked the bus times. The next one is at ten tonight, so you'd be in Montreal by about one in the morning."

When I didn't answer, she continued. "You know it's been such a hard year for Didier...why are you crying?"

"You deserve so much better than this."

"Are you sure you aren't hungry? You hardly ate."

"I'm not hungry, Bri."

"I guess that's how you English stay so tall and skinny. But Didier likes an ass on his women." She slapped a mosquito on my arm but caught it too late. I rubbed the bead of blood with my thumb and it smeared.

She said, "If only you'd tried to get rid of the fish."

THE END

I woke up not as unhappy as I thought I'd be.

My foam mattress was about two inches thick. I could feel the uneven floorboards underneath. The bed, if it could be called one, was squeezed into an alcove in front of a crooked, curtainless window. In the room was the mattress, a rocking chair covered with orange Muppet fur, and a bookcase on which were neatly folded items of my scavenged wardrobe. A couple pairs of underwear. Jeans. Some shirts. My alarm clock clicked its muted battery-operated metronome, timing the morning's pale yellow beams, which flooded through ashen maple branches in a pre-spring stream, all show-offy triangular angles, no heat.

I got up. Careful not to wake my waitress roommate, I made coffee, heated soy milk in her saucepan and sat at her round oak table. I kept thinking I saw my cat in the corners of the room, but she wasn't there yet. The coffee, an entire percolator's worth, was thick and good and my favourite part of the day.

The sky clouded over and started to spit as I got ready to leave. It was an hour's walk through the Plateau, the ghetto, and then downtown to the lofty temple-design Bank of Montreal-turned-boutique. To the soundtrack of lounge mixes, I sold dishes and sauces and sweaters and bath bombs and lampshades and placemats and wine openers. Everything in the store was singularly beautiful—a song of every thing. It's true about the truth in beauty—how, for instance, a Stelton jug in burnt orange melamine expresses like no other thing the quiddity of the cylinder.

After six hours, and congratulations from my manager, I walked under rain turned to pouring. I was too poor for an umbrella. My only shoes were worn through the way I imagined a child of the Depression's would've been, leather peeling from the soles, toes poking through the top.

Uphill along Clark, water rushed over the sidewalks, over the gutters.

It wasn't thunder season, yet.

I was cooking scrambled eggs and rice when my roommate came in, banging open all the windows, saying my dinner had smelled up the place.

She stood behind me as I stirred at the stove, fanning the back door open and closed with vehement arm motions, effectively replacing the smell of cooking eggs with the smell of backyard ice melting into thawing earth, a hovering, molecular hint of green, buds paining their way out, fresh as alfalfa, tremulous chartreuse.

I shivered.

CHEZ SERGE

He says, "I'm sorry I don't have any tea and oranges."

It would be hard for Serge to have either since he doesn't have groceries or anything to boil water in. He's one of those proud bachelors, a lifer, from a generation of men who never learned to take care of themselves properly—every lunch is a poutine and two-dog deal, every dinner is delivered in a greased box. But it's a nice line to throw around, even if it has been used before.

Serge hands Louise a Mason jar half-filled with maple syrup-coloured scotch. It's good scotch. It's expensive. Louise holds the jar to her chest. She shoulders against the bathroom door-jamb, eyes shutting from some kind of sleepy nervousness. "I don't know why you're here with me," Serge says. He folds a striped towel on the side of the tub. She's getting the bed and breakfast treatment tonight. She's been coming over every Thursday after his hockey practices for a couple of weeks, *rien de spécial* about *ce soir*.

"Come on," she says. She yawns. She has a sip of her drink.

The air steams, perfumed by the sweet and sour smell of synthetic kelp that foams thickly in the bathwater.

"But I'm so ugly," Serge says. His accent distorts the vowels into an elongated whine. *Uuuugl-ie*. She watches his face empty itself of expression. He's used to hating himself, she thinks, to the feeling of numbness it provokes.

He puts her glass on the tiled floor. He takes off her wet sweater, pulls down her pants, tugs off the mismatched socks that stink of her Salvation Army sneakers. He lifts her into the tiny rectangular tub. She lets him do this, the way you do when you're a kid and you pretend to be asleep when you're really just drowsy—to feel the weightless comfort of someone levering you against their torso.

☙❧

When Louise wakes, Serge is still asleep. He snores like someone's father. She lies there freezing until the alarm goes off around ten. Serge gets out of bed to go to the bathroom, stepping over the pile of hair he cut a few weeks ago that feathers out over the hardwood floor like the remnants of a moulting blackbird. He comes back in, pulls on a pair of shorts and a shirt with embroidery along the buttonholes. He tells her she's more beautiful in the morning; he coughs phlegm into some toilet paper and roots deep into his nose for a load of dried-up skin and snot. He tells her that one day his nose will rot off his face. He says they should have breakfast. "Did you want to borrow my toothbrush? I promise no other woman has used it."

Louise slaloms ahead of Serge on her sister's old bike as he greets folks stepping out of their curly-staired apartments—some PG-13 version of *Sesame Street*'s "These Are the People in Your Neighbourhood."

"Mario's so pretty he sleeps with all the girls on the block,"

Serge says. Mario is pretty, in the raised-by-a-single-mom, embraces-all-of-womanity, wears-a-bone-and-hemp-necklace way. Mario waves at Louise and winks at Serge.

At the restaurant, Christelle, the waitress, flirts with Serge. "Give me a kiss," she says, and he obliges. She balances two plates on her left arm.

"*Salut,* how's your baby?"

"Yeah, okay, better. She just needed some cough syrup, finally."

Christelle gets all the mornings after. Louise wonders what Serge's gaggle looks like. Once she brought it up and he answered that she shouldn't care what other people thought. She worries as much as she is curious of their separate and combined effects. Are they a variety pack or shades of a flavour?

They choose a table at the end of the room. Serge takes the chair and lets Louise sit on the bench against the wall. They switch places every time, each preferring a view of the restaurant to the feeling of movement behind them.

The waitress asks if Louise needs a menu, as if she didn't eat here all the time, as if she was trying to snub Louise into transience. Louise orders the same thing she gets every Friday. Two eggs, scrambled, and pumpernickel toast. No potatoes, extra bacon.

"*Café?*"

"*S'il vous plaît.*" Louise is jealous of the waitress' prototypical Parisian style, her arrogant accent, her big brown eyes—what the French would call black eyes.

The waitress pours a coffee for Louise and holds out a bowl of café au lait for Serge. She has huge hands.

"I can't believe you drink that stuff," Serge says. "You should have gotten an espresso."

"This is cheaper."

"But it sucks."

"I get free refills."

"I'm inviting you."

She shrugs and has a sip. "I didn't know you were going to."

In public, Serge insists on speaking to her theatrically in English, as if she doesn't speak French, as if it weren't her own mutter tongue. "I like your photographs," he announces from his diaphragm. "I'm not just saying that because I'm fucking you, either."

Her stomach cramps with shame. She can't believe he said "fucking you" in front of all these people. She's his tacky CN Tower souvenir: *Regardez, mesdames et messieurs, ce spécimen du Canada anglais.* Yours to Discover.

They're eating eggs and digging into the basket of toast when Serge says that he thinks his friend Antoine is starting to like her. She thinks of Antoine as the Gregor Samsa sidekick. She lets Serge's comment slide. But Serge has stopped eating and he looks at her, he ogles her, trying to drive the point home. Here, *mesdames et messieurs,* is a moment to pause. Her participation is required. She picks her line carefully.

"You mean he's attracted to me."

"Yeah."

"I don't know."

"I do. I was watching you guys all night. I don't want to get in the way of love, but you have to let me know if you start seeing each other."

Is it jealousy, maligned generosity? Is she supposed to fuck them both? She says she doesn't want to fuck Antoine.

"Well you might, and if you do you'll probably fall in love, and then you'll have to tell me."

They've worked out some kind of man's loyalty with regards to boundaries and women. Women like countries to be staked out by soldiers. This is mine, that is yours. Her own pulsions entirely immaterial to their gentlemanly understanding.

"I'd choose him over me. But you have to tell me if something happens."

"Jesus. It's not gonna happen."

There's something continental, something genteel in Antoine's manner that relaxes Louise, particularly in contrast to Serge's roughhousing. Antoine always shares his dessert with her; he lights her cigarettes. But maybe it's just that he acts normal, albeit in a voyeuristically deferential manner. They can speak—in French—about books or work, the way that people do.

The couple next to them work at TQS; they're talking about renewing contracts and buying property. Louise doesn't know why they're not at the office. She feels self-conscious that they might be listening to her conversation. Of course they are, they're less than a foot away. Serge says, "I don't know why there are so many people here on a weekday."

Louise piles bacon on the back of her fork with her knife. Serge eats like a lumberjack, uses his fork to cut his ham, takes some of the potatoes they'd given her by mistake from her plate. "You sure you don't want to try them?"

"I don't like potatoes."

"What?"

"What? I'm thinking about what you said."

"Trying it on for size?"

"No."

"Then what?"

"I don't feel like telling you here."

"You can't just say that."

"Fine. You do what you want. I know you see other women." He told her on their second night together that there are three, including her. She guesses a fourth in Rimouski, probably irregular others. "But don't start pushing me on your friends under some moral guise—that 'he's a better man than me' shit." She remembers the time she went for the friend instead. "I'm not in love with Antoine," she says. She doesn't know if she's in love with Serge, or if she's just moved by his throbbing, certain pain; if his brokenness just makes him seem more vital than anyone else. Her ex used to tell her she had a persecution complex—except it wasn't an invented one. She used to try to absorb her parents' blame, to sponge up its vinegary wounds. The *toi t'as pas de cœur*. The traitor shit, the general degenerateness. But sometimes she'd break up the scapegoat routine. She discharged a vocabulary of remembered injuries with the precision of advancing militia. In their own ways, she and Serge had made their families pay for disregarding them, and their eyes caught each other's smarting intelligence the way headlights refract against a bike's reflector. A braise, a quick synthetic spark in the dark.

"It's hard not to want it, the house, the fence, the three tulips," he says. An uninventive, childish landscape—tulips with points to match the kinds of houses no one lived in.

Louise is determined not to provoke him. She's humbled when she thinks how arrogantly she once flaunted love. Her previous relationship somehow became a prize of merit, a clear delineation between a solitary childhood and adult life cut in gold around her finger.

"I never expected those things," she says. "Maybe just a honeymoon." Some short respite bracketed from the straight-as-an-interstate-headed-west sentence of the quotidian. She looks over their plates of orange and honeydew rinds, checks the time. She's running late for her shift at the hospital.

At the cash, Christelle shows Serge the run in her stockings, and where it ends, just under the hem of her sparkly jean skirt. Her fishnets are apple green and the lozenges of string and skin lend her legs a scaled texture. She giggles.

"So, *euh*, what did you guys eat? I forget."

Serge leans his weight against the counter and says what he says every Friday morning. "Soda crackers, some water, a few napkins, straws..." It's a shtick, it's kind of stupid, but Louise still thinks it's funny. So does Christelle. Serge's closed-mouth grin levers between the two women who look up at him familiarly.

NUMBER 42

The punk passed out when they stuck her with the catheter. *Sarrau*-clad technicians flocked around her like garbage-diving gulls. The girl came to and squeezed out globby baby tears. The techs pushed strands of jello-pink hair off her face with a sterilized wet cloth and lifted her to a dentist chair at the back of the lab. A technician moved to sit in front of me. She snapped on a fresh pair of latex gloves. The punk's collapse made me want to *sacrer mon camp*. I needed the thousand bucks; I asked the technician her name. "I'm Nurse Two. Hold out your arm." She was almost beautiful. A few traces of cystic acne. Pupils that seeped into brown irises.

A bruise smudged the inside of my elbow from last night's tests. Nurse Two slapped around for a new vein. "Bothered by needles?" She was used to people chickening out and slid into condescension. "Do you want me to show you how it works?" She dangled tentacles of transparent tubes and jabbered at me. I squeezed a yellow ball with a smiley face in my fist. Nurse Two drove a malleable hose up my vein. Twin taps sprouted orange knobs from my forearm. Blood bubbled at the top. "You're done. Number 43! Number 43!"

I shuffled down to the cafeteria in my untied sneakers. Subjects

25 to 50 milled about, cradling their cathetered limbs in sling-like hugs. We waited for our doses of cholesterol treatment. Episodes of *Têtes à claques* played in a loop of googly eyes and tits on the TV hitched beside the kitchen elevator. Felt like being an old-ager in a home. I sat in my assigned chair. I was Number 42. Orderlies wheeled in carts and fed each of us a pill. The room filled with the sound of intermittent "aaaahs" as our palates and tongues were inspected to make sure we'd swallowed them.

The technicians set up their suction rounds. Nurse Three jammed a tube into the catheters. The catheters had fuchsia-tinted splash guards to contain the blood. Nurse Two rolled in with the syringes. An orderly daubed off spillage with alcohol swabs. All this organization before six a.m. I bled into vials that were labelled and shelved into trays loaded with ice cubes. The rhythm of splashing release began to feel pleasurable, like the gush of a long-awaited piss after a car ride. My blood whirred and thrummed against plastic over and over to the sound of alarms beeping at five-minute intervals. Number 41, beside me, was a woman who wore a mullet and Phentex slippers without any sense of irony. She leaned over her chair and almost into my lap. She told Nurse Two, "I love blood!" with affected fasci-nation, clearly enjoying being the subject of such scrutiny.

There was some coagulation action in my catheter about an hour into the procedures. Nurse Three, exasperated, tightened my tourniquet with a quick pull at the strap and jabbed fresh holes into my veins with a large pin. It hurt.

"Sensitive, are you?"

My heart beat against the daisy-covered tourniquet.

"Look at this clot!" said one nurse to the other, pointing out a floating scab in the vial.

Number 43, a big, bearded guy from British Columbia, told me how he was going to buy an Xbox with the cash reward. "And I think I'll be fine to give blood, now. I used to be so scared of needles."

"Cool," I said.

I guessed I wasn't in the placebo group because I started to feel bad. A kung fu movie blasting from the TV made it worse. I wanted to barf; I was freezing. The orderlies said they couldn't let me leave my chair to get my hoodie—I'd need to wait another four hours.

They asked me how I felt. "I feel nauseous and a little cold."

"How do you spell nauseous?" asked Nurse Two.

❧

After a while the orderlies handed out cups of grape juice. They stood over us to watch that we drank to the last drop and they took notes. Janitors mopped up the bloodstains around our feet. Number 41 sweated through her clothes. She started freaking out about how the grape juice was disgusting and she didn't want to drink it. The orderlies told her she had to. She drained her cup, sniffling.

After the snack hoopla I was permitted to lift my ass off the plastic chair. I called my girlfriend from one of the public phones. It was stuck to a cubbyhole in front of a window that looked out over some autoroutes. The receiver stank of sweat. A guy in track pants bragged on the phone beside me that this series of drugs were easy on him. "Last time they weighed my puke in a bag!" The man looked like he made a career of pharmaceutical testing without ever spending the rewards on his teeth. Meanwhile my girlfriend was yelling that she couldn't believe I was doing this and what if I had totally fucked up my whole life being a guinea pig for a drug company. I watched some woman take the tattooed man's phone. Her hair was pulled into a bun—just another day at the office. She wore heels. "*Si, si amor. Te quiero.*"

⚭

At night, after the orderlies watched me eat my entire portion of *pâté chinois* and chicken soup and tinned pears, I lay on my rubber mattress on the metal bunk bed underneath Number 43. Nothing—not the yellow glow of the emergency lights, not the wheezing ventilation, could keep me from sleeping. At five a.m. they slammed on the fluorescent lights. We lined up by the bathrooms for our urine tests, rubbing our heads and yawning.

"How come my piss is a different colour than everybody else's?" asked the toothless man, comparing his orange urine to the succession of yellow beakers on the table. His piss looked like one of those fertilized eggs you get sometimes; the liquid was shot through with ribbons of red. "If I was sick, you'd tell me, right?"

"*Oui, Monsieur.* You would not have been accepted for the study if you were sick."

A new technician told me not to let my genitals touch the receptacle this time. I trickled carefully into my cup. The container was so warm that I was embarrassed to hand it over to the Laval-pretty orderly who sat at her stand with her cups in tidy rows, as if she were selling us all lemonade.

MANICURE

That fish is a caricature of a fish, thought Miriam. The fish was a cartoony violet and its bright pink gills looked as fake as glued-on sequins. It had at least three jowly chins and protruding google eyes.

The tank, maybe three feet by two, seemed a tight fit for such a large creature. The fish wasn't quite a foot long, but it was at least four inches fat. Could it even turn? Or was it just marking time, fanning its fins in place? Someone had taped a poster of a rainforest on the back of the aquarium; the fish would never know it was in a Walmart. A handwritten sign on the front of the tank read, "Please do not touch the fish." And, beneath this message, in French, "*Ne touchez pas le poison*." Do not touch the poison.

Chantel, Miriam's manicurist, returned to Miriam's table with a bottle of burgundy polish. "This looks very nice on small nails," she told Miriam, arching her tattooed-on eyebrows. "Such small nails," she clucked, taking Miriam's right hand and resting it in a plastic bowl of scented, soapy water. Miriam bit her nails while she read, while she worried. It was ridiculous to even attempt to pretty them up. They would just look overdone, she scolded her-self, like she was trying too hard. But then, she thought, coddling her vanity might be an inducement to rein in her bad habits. Miriam looked up and caught her reflection in the mirrored wall. She saw just how plain she looked under the fluorescent lights; she looked back down at her hands. A heavyset woman in her late sixties took the chair beside her. The manicurist seated before her started sanding down her acrylic nails with what looked like a whirring, rotating saw. Nail dust flew everywhere. Chantel took Miriam's hand. She said, "It's so cold!"

"It is cold," Miriam agreed, happy for a distraction. She knew it was rude to keep watching as her neighbour's nails got shaved down into dainty, sliced-in-half almonds.

Chantel's tiny hands massaged oil into Miriam's palms and along her wrists. The motion was overly familiar. To assuage her discomfort at the intimacy with Chantel, Miriam imagined that she knew these hands, that they were friends. She tried to conjure the person who might touch Chantel's hands with such tenderness but came up empty. A generic, smiling man face.

The woman beside her had her middle finger stuck in a shot glass full of acetone.

"I thought I could go fishing by now! I thought spring was here!" Chantel said. "But it's too cold for fishing."

"Ice fishing?" Miriam asked.

"Not ice fishing."

"Where do you fish?"

"Near Champlain Bridge. Or Jacques-Cartier Bridge. Or Pierrefonds," she said.

"How often do you fish?" asked Miriam.

"Once every two days. I love to fish!"

"Do you eat the fish?"

"Yes."

Miriam moved her right hand over to a fan rigged into the melamine desk, and Chantel started to work on her left. Miriam's arms were crossed uncomfortably, and she noticed her neighbour's posture mirrored her own.

The shop's owner came in from outside. He sat on a pedicure chair, watching the fish in the tank. He was on his phone, speaking in a language Miriam couldn't identify.

"So what do you do in the winter?" Miriam asked Chantel. "About the fish?"

"I buy fish. It is very expensive," said Chantel. "I have three tanks at home. For big fish, middle fish, little fish. So many fish!"

"Is it a lot of work to keep so many aquariums?" Miriam asked, watching as Chantel paused her nail polish application. She put down the bottle of varnish and picked up a pair of pliers to pluck a thread that had travelled from Miriam's sweater into the polish. The pliers were still jammed with the cuticles Chantel had clipped from Miriam's fingers. Miriam wondered if the pieces of skin would flake into the polish, but they didn't.

"It is a lot of work. Every two days, I clean the tanks. Some people say you can wait a week, but I never wait a week. As soon as I see a small thing I have to clean it."

Chantel couldn't pluck the thread out of the polish, which was starting to gum. Instead, she applied another coat of polish over the thread, and it disappeared.

"The colour is nice," said Miriam.

"Yes, a good colour for small nails. Do you fish?"

"No. But maybe I should."

Chantel gestured that she should shape her hands into claws and aim them closer to the fans.

"You have to have a license. Or..."

"You'll get in trouble?"

"Yes."

"Like a fine?"

"Yes."

"I should try sometime," said Miriam, who had never before imagined eating fish caught from the Saint Lawrence.

She wondered what the Saint Lawrence fish would taste like—like real fish, or like toilet-bowl fish? She wondered what someone who spent every other day by the highway, under the huge bridge that connected the island to the South Shore, at the part of the Saint Lawrence where the rapids rip up the blues and greys, what that person saw of the city she never did.

"You can go now," Chantel told her after a while. "I will help you with your coat."

"Thank you so much," said Miriam. She stood up.

Her coat was a bulky, sporty kind of foul weather jacket. She remembered being on an internet date with some sound tech guy who had told her, "I could never date a woman who wore a sports coat." She sighed. It was her warmest coat. She'd bought it at the big second-hand store nearby.

She watched herself putting her coat on in the mirror. Her workday makeup had worn off. Her fingernail stubs, she noticed as she fixed a hidden pin in her scarf at her temple, shone dark, luminous maroon.

Miriam exited the salon, walked past the automatic doors of the Walmart and stepped outside into the black and white landscape of the empty parking lot. Slivers of silver ice refracted the lot's bright stadium lights. Across the empty expanse, a lineup of cars at the Burger King, their collective exhaust fogging the air around them. A gust of wind tore through the open space with such ferocity that Miriam was forced to take a step backwards. Her breath caught in her throat; her eyes pricked, then teared. She coughed.

Miriam stepped carefully over the icy sidewalk and crossed the highway overpass over to the metro station. She pushed the station's heavy, wind-funnelling swinging door and wiped her still-watering eyes and frozen nose on her sleeve. She took the escalator down three flights, scanned her pass past the STM officer in his aquarium, and rode the few stops north to Côte-Vertu.

DIRECTIONS

It rained my first day in Bonn. I was stuck at the train station. My phone cards didn't work. Or I was too dumb to figure them out. Bulked down by a giant suitcase I had to tip and roll, I went in and out of the station's stores, soliciting assistance. Tellers contracted politely away. *Ich spreche kein Deutsch.*

Back at the platform a woman loaned me her cell and friends soon scooped me in their compact VW. An apartment. Babies. Stories of hard days at the office. Toddlers crashing into knees requesting beads, dollies, cheese, and apple juice. I sat on the floor. They crawled over their friend from Canada and laughed at my French accent.

Finalement, l'heure de la sieste.

With directions folded into my wallet I left the house. I didn't have far to go. Past the castle. Past the flawlessly aligned corridor of trees and cordoned greens. Past the pond, where even the ducks nested bucolically beneath a footbridge, and there—. A statue of Beethoven in a square. A toy store where Pinocchio's elephantine nose peaked over the cobbled street. A downtrodden pastry shop where old people hunched over their hands to maw almond croissants, sandwiching brown paper bags under their armpits, exhaling against the glass. A cumbersome series of grabs. The bags, the windows, their collective respirations fogging before their faces. They wore calf-length trench coats and lumpy hats. A staggered reiteration of costumes, replicas of morose retirees out of a Kafka bureaucracy.

Rain reappeared. Not the pitter-patter kind of rain, but the smearing against the windows kind. Like the cluster at the windows, I ate my almond croissant. Despite its dense sweetness, I ate it. I had said I would eat it. I sat on a plastic seat attached to a plastic table. I didn't want to give up my spot to one of the old folks who shifted uncomfortably from one stout heel to the next.

Wait. I was eating an apple something. Strudel. The almond croissant was another day. The next day. And I watched the people in the pane and the rain falling over Beethoven's statue and chewed and swallowed and felt like an idiot. You know when you have been had. When you see that you've been childish and for a while you just feel shitty about not knowing that you were so stupid—you don't want to think yourself capable of being so stupid. I don't want to throw around a word like shame. It's too punishing. Regret is too nostalgic. I sat there thinking neither of those words, just—*I am such an asshole*.

When the rain stopped I vacated my seat and was immediately replaced.

I followed the directions from my wallet in reverse back to the apartment.

COLONY

She dreamed again that she was in a huge, ritzy bathtub. The water was too hot. A little hotter and she could've been boiled alive.

There were people on the other side of the door. They didn't live there; they were visitors, too. They knew she was washing and one of them was waiting for her to finish. She tried to enjoy the warmth of the water. Then she noticed the water had begun to fill with blood. She looked over her arms and legs to see where she was injured. She realized the blood was pouring out from inside of her. She felt something ungainly slip out. It was lumpy and difficult to grasp in the bathwater but finally she had it in her hands: an adult-sized human heart. Its arteries spurted blood like a fountain. Her own heart pounded. She panicked. She started to yell.

A man from the other side of the door entered the room. He was tall and calm. She could feel his concern. She was ashamed for him to see her naked, covered in blood, holding the spongy, spurting heart. He lifted her out of the tub and wrapped her in a dirty towel—the towel belonged to the people who usually lived in the house—and led her out of the room, heart in hands. The man cleaned the bath, scrubbing it of blood; finally, the heart ran out of blood. She didn't recall disposing of it—she just looked down and it was no longer there.

☙❧

When she was a little girl she had hoped to have the full twelve, the whole package, the full set. Twelve kids of her own. The twelfth, as promised, would go on to study. Fully funded. She'd see them off from the port, the ship's square, silver sail blinking away and off.

The rest of them, the eleven and her match, would, of course, never leave. They would have married the earth. It was the tradition. The arid soil, this dirt, the cold, dry earth was theirs, their people's. They mined its rocks and cooked its minerals. They were the pioneers. Their people were the most desperate and the most courageous.

But she hasn't had any children. Her life has been all sweat and no fruit. She has not taught these lessons; only miscarried her own heart.

EMBOUCHURE

I wasn't Lars' first choice. I looked a little like the girl he really liked except she was more athletic and I was less friendly. No matter: I was more into his friend Krzysztof. But, then, as now, I knew you just have to take what comes your way.

Lars used to pick me up after my late-night shift at McDonald's. I'd get into his mother's white Toyota after filling up all the ketchup stations and hosing down the fry vats. The fry vats fogged up my glasses and made me gag from the reek of boiled meat grease.

There was a customer who was always after me to stop wearing my glasses. He said they made me ugly. They did, but he shouldn't have said anything about it. He was gross in an unwashed truck driver way. He came in every Monday night to buy a hamburger patty with extra onions for his dog.

Lars and I drove to the beach after my shifts. I stank up the car with my oily purple uniform, and he played with my stinky oily hair. He said he liked how it was soft. We fumbled around outside, two virgins who didn't like each other a whole lot excited by proximity.

The first time I went down on Lars was to the soundtrack of *Dances with Wolves*. We were in the basement of his parents' suburban split-level, hidden in a storage closet beside the Ping-Pong table.

The closet was my idea. I was worried his parents or his little brother Elias would hear something sexy going on. Lars lay there, sprawled in garbage bags full of baby clothes, blue skivvies tangled inside the track pants around his ankles. It was all right. After a while, he went back to his bedroom and I slept in my uniform on the downstairs sofa.

Next morning, he made me pancakes. We sat at his family's dining table, under a chandelier constructed of model Viking ships. The pancakes were bitter; we sprinkled powdered sugar over them. I was a little round, then. Not fat, or even chubby, just padded out in the curvy parts. Lars' mom, Solveig, a tiny woman-child with a childish whisper, sat beside me and told me not to eat so much. She said if I ate only grapefruit for a week, I'd lose all my baby fat. She said it was very slimming, grapefruit. Solveig dressed in combinations of polyester pinks, nurse clothes plucked from the 1960s. She gloated that she used to tell her sons that she made the sun rise and set, that she could punish them by refusing to allow the dawn to break if they watched too much TV. She told me it was okay that Lars and Elias worked at the video store. They were old enough to realize that porn wasn't necessarily setting a good example, but it was good business sense. And after all, their country had been the first country to legalize pornography.

Solveig didn't know that Lars had recurring nightmares about the video store. Several times a week he'd dream the popcorn machine overflowed and overflowed, like that Hans Christian Andersen fairy tale about the porridge pot. He'd dream he was behind the shower curtain that divided adult from new releases, up to his knees in salted buttered corn, bailing it like bilge. All those neon-lit pictures of bodies crowding him in, using open videocassette cases like buckets till he choked himself awake.

ILLUMINATION

The road stretched out in front of them, into melting tar mirages and then on again. They drove towards the setting sun, towards where it dropped off behind the road. The asphalt was smooth, black; the yellow line down the middle was freshly squeezed fluorescent sunset yellow. The soft shoulders were soft. The grasses on either side of the road striated occasionally into bald badland dirt patches, broken up then quickly enlivened again by field and grass and or wild bush. As they progressed along South Dakota's I-71, the dry tracts spread and multiplied across the topography. The dry strips stretched and touched each other until it was the grass that became an inconsistent surprise; it went on like that until the landscape was entirely dusty, hard, and lunar.

Geneviève and Cheryl and Malik drove with all four windows down. The wind was a deafening, soothing, blinding hush. Cheryl leaned her head out the passenger window and waved her ACE-bandaged arm against the wind. The whooshes of air dipped and peaked according to the placement of her arm in the window's frame.

It was August. The light didn't last as long as it had when they'd driven in the other direction, but the deep-lit indigo night still glowed until eight p.m. And after they'd parked, the stars poked out; they shone so bright that the trio could see well enough to pitch their two-person tent on the hard ground without using their flashlights. They'd paid their camping fee by the honour system, slipping an envelope of cash into a box near the front gate.

It was a long weekend and the park was crowded. Cars packed as densely as a mall parking lot at Christmastime. Though, of course, the view was better. People quieted for the night, and while some still milled about they spoke softly. The occasional dog barked and the odd car door opened and closed as campers put away their gear and packed it in for the night.

Geneviève, who was the only one who couldn't drive, took up dinner preparation. She propped up the stove on the campsite's wooden picnic table and screwed in a bottle of propane. She found a tap outdoors by the toilets, filled up the pot with water, and brought it back to their site. She lit a match, turned on the element, set it to boil and got the pasta out of a big plastic container from the back of the car. She went back to the tap with a couple of water bottles. She tipped some iced tea powder into them and then shook them hard. She was aware of the noisiness of her actions, the way the sounds of everything she touched resonated across the open, airy campsite.

Malik lay down in the backseat of the car, legs dangling out of the open door. He'd been doing most of the driving since Cheryl sprained her wrist at the championship in Michigan. Cheryl wasn't happy with the way the trip was turning out.

"Here you go." Geneviève handed Cheryl and Malik each a bottle of iced tea. Malik sat up, pushed his glasses up his nose with a knuckle. "Thanks," he said, taking it from her. Cheryl sat in the passenger seat with her eyes closed, her long, thick black plait lying diagonally across her sports bra like a seatbelt, resting in a fiddlehead curl by her bellybutton. She said nothing, feigning sleep. Geneviève placed the bottle by Cheryl's muddy, sandaled feet and went to check on the noodles.

Malik came up to her as she was draining the noodles, and mixed the two packs of K.D. powder into the pot. He took a couple of sachets of pepper, scavenged from a diner someplace in Montana, and added them for flavour.

Geneviève cut up a couple of bell peppers and pulled out a bag of pre-cut orange carrots. She called to Cheryl, telling her dinner was ready. Geneviève spooned the macaroni and cheese into three bowls and piled the cutlery in the middle of the table, crossways against the table's slats.

Cheryl got out of the car and walked over. She sat down, avoiding eye contact with Geneviève and Malik. She grabbed a fork and took a stab at her macaroni.

It was an RV-heavy site. They could see campers locked in their humming air-conditioned bubbles while blue lights flickered across their drawn curtains.

Geneviève felt the air turning cold. She untied her fleece from around her waist and pulled it over her head. It caught briefly on her glasses.

Cheryl said she was cold but didn't move to get her sweater.

Geneviève made a point of grabbing a handful of peppers and carrots. "No one wants these?"

Malik said, "Hey, Cheryl, do you want me to get you your hoodie? Do you need another Tylenol?"

Malik didn't answer Geneviève; he went to the car to get Cheryl her bottle of painkillers.

Cheryl said, "Look at the stars."

Geneviève, obligingly, looked up. There were a lot.

A very tall, thin man walked in close to them, crossing over the threshold of their site, his feet landing hard and crunching against the pebbles and dirt.

"Hello over there!" he bellowed too loudly, from too close.

Malik came out from the car with the painkillers, which he handed to Cheryl. "Hi," he answered back.

"Hey," Geneviève said, not liking the look of the man. Brand spanking new safari outfit. One of those weird broad hats, even at night. Sunglasses around his neck on a brand new rubber cord.

"I see y'all are from Canada," the stranger said, pointing to their plates.

"Yup," Malik answered.

"Y'all must be excited about the Nordiques moving over to Colorado."

"Not so much, no," said Geneviève.

"Why not?" asked the stranger.

"Because they've been around since 1972 and I'm not so stoked about them being sold to some American franchise." She'd said as much dozens of times in the car; her words sounded rehearsed, singsong, schoolmarmy.

"That's amazing!" said the man. "I'd never have guessed you wouldn't be excited for their new opportunity in America."

"Oh well," said Cheryl. "At least they kept the team together."

"And they'll make more money! We sure are excited. I live in Colorado," he said, adding, "I'm Randy."

Of course you are, thought Geneviève.

"Hey there," said Cheryl. "Nice to meet you."

"What are you guys doing over here?"

"We're headed home," said Malik. "To Vancouver."

"Where were you all at?" asked Randy.

"We were in Michigan. For an Ultimate competition."

"A what kind of competition?"

"Ultimate. We play with discs. A Frisbee football game?"

"Isn't that something!" the man said.

Malik smiled gently at him. "We came in sixth. Not so great, but not bad." Malik was studying to be a high school teacher. He could speak kindly to people who didn't know how to behave, and he knew how to look people in the eye and not feel depleted by the exertion of over-explaining something.

"Well, that's great. Good for you. Good to stay active," said the man. "Well, I'll let you guys eat your din-dins. Be sure to look for fossils in the morning."

"Maybe we will," said Geneviève.

They finished their macaroni without speaking.

When they were done, Geneviève walked back over to the pump and filled the pot up again with water. She squeezed in some soap and put the pot back on the stove. The water came to a simmer, and the smell of lemony dish detergent wafted into the night air, mingling with the smell of dirt and juniper bushes.

Malik came out with a flashlight for the table and a dishtowel over his shoulder. "I'll dry," he said.

Cheryl opened up the back of the car to grab her sleeping bag and her sleeping mat, which was just a roll of bubble wrap they'd picked up at a Canadian Tire outside of Regina on their way out. She hunkered down in her corner of the tent. Geneviève could hear the vague sound of her Discman spinning the soundtrack of *Reservoir Dogs*.

Malik and Geneviève finished the dishes and put everything back in the car.

"Want to go for a walk?" said Malik, taking Geneviève's hand.

"Sure."

They crunched along the ground out past the toilets, past the information centre, their eyes growing used to the depth of the darkening night. Crickets creaked around them and the grass flicked against their legs from time to time as they stepped along the uneven path at the top of the badland. They stopped and sat down on the ground.

"Orion," said Malik.

"Big Dipper," said Geneviève.

"Little Dipper."

"Venus."

"North Star."

"Mars or satellite?" she said, pointing to something reddish that blinked from behind wisps of trailing cloud over the stars.

"Satellite. No. Mars. I don't know."

"Want to find someplace more private?"

"I don't know. I didn't bring anything. Maybe just for a little bit."

Malik held out his hand and she took it. She was a little scared of heights, and she stepped carefully down the hill into the folds of the cracked earth.

"I hope there aren't any coyotes here," she said.

"There probably are."

"I hope they don't visit."

"Me too."

They found a place to sit together that seemed remote enough. Malik held out his arm and she sat beside him and he put his arm around her. They hadn't camped anywhere with showers for a few days and both of them were a little sticky, a little hairy, a little rank. But it was pleasant. Real human flavour, Geneviève called it. It was nice to know what someone could really smell like when they didn't go through the ritual of detergents.

They exchanged macaroni-and-cheese-flavoured kisses, their sunburnt faces smelling of wind and sun. They made out in a sleepy, friendly way for a while and drew apart. They sat leaning shoulder to shoulder.

"Cheryl's pretty pissed," said Geneviève.

"My brother said if I was going on this trip I'd wind up dating one of the two women—he said it was inevitable. I didn't believe him but I guess he was right."

"We have to stop kissing in the tent. I know she can hear us."

"We always wait till she's asleep. She can't hear anything."

"She's just pretending. It's gross when you think about it. We're not being cool." Geneviève rubbed her face, feeling ashamed of herself and tired.

"It's not fair," Geneviève continued. "She thought this was going to be a trip with her two friends and now we're together and she's alone and has to drive with us for weeks." She moved her hand along and up his arm. She liked his Frisbee muscles.

"Yeah, it's not cool."

"Sometimes I wish you'd taken Tracy with you the way you'd planned, instead of me. Plus Tracy can drive. And this wouldn't have happened and everything would have been like before," she said.

"This is better."

Geneviève stiffened and looked over her shoulder. "Do you feel something?" she asked.

"I'm feeling something." He smiled at her.

"No, seriously. Do you feel like someone is watching us?"

"Geneviève. You have to get over it. Cheryl's not here. We're basically on the moon. No one's here. No one's watching us. Maybe a fox?"

"Wait—hang on, Malik. For real! I just feel really creepy right now. Hey—go away!" she said to the air around them.

"McKenzie," he said, referring to her by her last name, "who are you talking to?"

There was a click. Like a flicked switch?

Stadium-bright lights lit.

Bore into their eyes.

Geneviève couldn't make out the source of the immediate, intense brightness.

She could hear an engine. A high-pitched warble.

A hot feeling.

Like a nearby forest fire.

Close.

Orange and white. And whiter light.

Bright.

Sparks.

She couldn't breathe.

She couldn't feel Malik's arm.

Dirt blew into her eyes; she was unable to shut them. "What the fuck!" Malik yelled. But the sound didn't travel. It sounded like they were in a soundproof room.

Geneviève could feel herself trembling and shaking and maybe crying, too, she couldn't tell for sure. She felt like puking. There were geometric patterns on the edges of the bright light; they clicked like a kaleidoscope, around and around.

She saw fuchsia, orange, pink, mauve, violet.

Then all white again.

The heat from the engine (was it a fire?) gave the sensation of baking her.

She was becoming dehydrated.

She was turning into dirt.

She was smoking.

She was air-dried.

She was ash.

Her mouth was sand.

She couldn't breathe in. Or exhale.

She fell or lay down or collapsed.

She couldn't tell where her movements originated.

She felt rocks digging into her back.

She didn't know where Malik was, the light burned, she took shallow breaths, she tried to open her eyes.

Then she could blink.

The slowest blink.

Upward, creaking upward forever.

Down, friction, motioning down forever.

She kept her eyes shut and felt the easy pleasure of her body breathing, her body there with her inside it and breathing.

And it was night.

She kept squeezing her eyes. She saw stars under her lids. "I'm freezing," she said. Her mouth moved normally. Her legs were frozen. Because she was wearing shorts and it was night. She was fine. That was normal.

Malik was asleep on the ground beside her. He lay on his side, thumb in his mouth, his T-shirt riding up over the side of his ribs.

She pushed a button on her digital watch to check the time. It was almost four in the morning. They'd left the campsite at eleven. She roused herself slowly and shook Malik on the shoulder. "Wake up," she said. "Malik?"

Malik stirred then looked over at her. He sat up. "I have to go to the bathroom," he said. He got up tentatively then walked down the hill and out into a clearing and urinated onto the ground. Geneviève realized she also had to pee. She walked out near him, pulled down her pants and squatted.

"You should take them all the way off or you'll piss on yourself again," Malik said.

She nodded and took off her shorts and squatted. Her urine riveted against the dry, hard ground. She stepped out of its way and then put her shorts back on.

She went up to Malik and held out her hands. He took them.

"I feel weird," he said.

"Me, too. I think I have a migraine."

"What's that?" he said, pointing to her arm. There was a four-inch oblong shape indented into her flesh.

"I don't know. A rock? Maybe I fell asleep on a rock."

"It doesn't look like a rock did that."

"Maybe it's from a rock or maybe it's from some piece of junk on the ground. Maybe an arrowhead."

"It looks like a burn. A brand."

When she touched it, it ached. She definitely had a migraine coming. It rose from her neck and over her brow like a balaclava. She rubbed her temples and then the back of her neck with her thumbs.

Sunrise crept in. Geneviève and Malik went back to their make-out spot and sat down by where they'd slept. There was an outline of their prone bodies carved into the dirt. Maybe from wind, Geneviève thought. Maybe what happened was the wind piled up a little outline of their bodies as they slept. She didn't remember falling asleep. She brushed the outline with her fingers. It was dense, as if calcified. It felt both porous and skeletal, like coral. Like something that had been there from the glacial age.

Geneviève yawned. She was so tired. This dumb trip. She'd quit her nannying job for this dumb trip and she was almost out of money. She'd traded in her best friend for a boyfriend on this dumb trip, and he was going to go away to school in a few weeks anyways. This dumb trip to visit her parents in Saint-Boniface on the way but they hadn't really cared. She couldn't even play Ultimate and had had to sit on the sidelines making iced tea for everyone during the playoffs. She shouldn't have come.

Malik put his arm around Geneviève. They heard the desert stir. The wind pricked up and blew dust and sand over rocks and over itself. Small animals rustled just out of sight. The sparse landscape's short grasses rubbed against each other quietly. It was as if the desert whispered itself awake. Geneviève and Malik sat facing eastward and watched as the dawn light broke the lunar landscape out of its grey scale, as the sliver of sun crested over the white and orange horizon. The stars faded into the pinking sky, the mauving pinking oranging sky. The sounds grew louder and beyond them the campsite picked up, people opened and closed their camper doors, a fire started, a griddle, a baby cried, a dog barked.

The two got up. They brushed the dirt off the backs of their shorts and began to walk single file up towards their campsite.

"What happened to us last night?" said Geneviève.

"What?"

"I said, what happened to us last night?"

"It wasn't anything," said Malik.

He kept walking.

SPAM

Isaac said, "Baby, you taste like canned meat."

"What did you say?" said Caitlin, laughing. "Corned beef?"

And he said, "No, you're so sweet you taste like candy, baby."

It was a bullshit lie in service of a pity fuck. She could tell his heart wasn't in it. His face moved the way a stingray does on water. Skin like parachute cloth, muscles malleable from every fluctuating emotion.

Isaac tugged on his jeans with the holes at the knees she'd tried to sew up and he'd ripped through. Caitlin put on her dog-walking clothes. They went outside. It was April but snowy as February, winter hibernating long into spring. She walked him partway back to his place—a house he shared with five other people on the western edge of her neighbourhood. Isaac was saying, "I don't know if I'm making the right decision, I don't know if this is right," and she was saying, "What are you saying?"

They crossed Jean-Talon. Isaac leaned into an alley and puked once, twice. The sound of his big-man, baritone retching resonated as it hit a slush puddle. Caitlin's dog pulled at her leash. Isaac looked so sorrowful when he came back that it made Caitlin see-saw into a kind of giddiness in response. He slipped in the second-hand square-toed boots she'd bought him and as he tried to get his balance, his green K-way rode up over a little patch of hairy stomach flesh. Caitlin would miss his hairy stomach, she knew. He reached for her hand. He wanted to kiss her. Caitlin gave him a peck. Her dog pulled. She felt the tug in her arm socket.

Caitlin held the leash in one hand, in the other a yellow bag of the dog's sloppy, soft shit. There were no garbage cans around. Isaac pushed her against a garage door and they kissed. It wasn't so bad. She didn't notice his breath, she just felt small.

A waning moon hung over Saint-Zotique, by the Guatemalan bakery, over the soon-to-be-closed arts centre with its ugly Matisse-imitation nudes in its dépanneur-like corner window. "See ya," Isaac said, and lope-limped off.

Caitlin's dog strained against her leash, towards the corner of the building, where traces of dog piss lingered in graffiti scent tags.

CAST

Mornings are cold, but then the days glow and warm. I get up around five-ish, sunrise time, when the crows answer to one another in their caw-caw-caws from one pine's peak to the next on the sand and stone shore that ridges the Ottawa River. The river is wide here and some of its noises reach the cottage in a background trickle-rush.

In Montreal, Pearl stays in bed all day, eating Rice Krispies squares, catching the afternoon soap operas, and her room smells like sweaty sheets, claustrophobia, and something I think of as rancid doughnuts. All blanketed by her over-spritzed Lauren by Ralph Lauren perfume.

"She's not well," my dad says, like a refrain to a psalm, again and again, to my questions of, *Why is she mean, Why doesn't she like me, Why is she still in bed.* She's not well is the reason for this, for her fingernail scratches down my face, for the zealous hoarding of my Christmas presents—*This is mine!*—for the occasional tosses of my body into the kitchen cupboards, for the stealing of my jewellery, for rules about no jam-eating for me, for the constant cleaning assignments, for the stern punishments of my mistakes.

I tiptoe by her room while I clean the house so I don't bother

her all snug as a bug in her sick. Though I often disturb her without meaning to. It's as though my nervousness tricks me into making more mistakes. I bump over the cleaning supplies basket. Miss a dust bunny behind the sofa with the broom. Drop the mop.

Pearl will move the sofa into the centre of the room, point out a straggling piece of lint I've neglected, probably on purpose, she supposes, I was trying to get away with it, with a job half done. She'll explain about her headaches, ask me to make some popcorn, tell me not to forget to scrub the bathroom floor clean with her old toothbrush. Especially between the tiles. She will check on it when she feels up to it, later, after her soaps. She will have to show me how to vacuum the stairs all over again since I can't always be trusted to take my responsibilities seriously. She left her job as a high school principal in Oshawa for this, because of me, because I couldn't change schools, so now here she is. Do I understand.

Yes.

Vacuuming. How it works is you take the attachment off the hose and you suck the back part of the staircase and the stair itself in an L-motion. There are seventeen stairs from the second floor to the ground floor of our house in Montreal. There are thirteen from the ground floor to the basement. It takes a while to vacuum all the Ls. You have to be patient. LLLLL is the whine of the vacuum cleaner. It wants to resist, but like me, it can't.

⊙⅊⊙

At the cottage, Pearl gets up early. Not at dawn, but well before nine. She makes us both coffee in a 1950s percolator. She makes hers a café au lait because of her osteoarthritis, for which she mixes powdered milk in a plastic container and heats it up in a saucepan. Warming powdered milk smells like barf. Like the second time you barf, when you're upchucking really old digested yogourt from your stomach.

We eat toasted slices of white bread from the gas station halfway to Pembroke and spread homemade blueberry jam bought from the church rummage sale in town. We don't talk. Pearl reads the *Ottawa Citizen* or the *Pembroke Daily Observer*, her long, freckled legs scissor-crossed in her chair. That is, one leg under her butt, and the other stretched elegantly in front of her. Even though she spends most of her time cooped up inside, she has a svelte, voluptuous, sexy body. Juicy. Like she's thinking about sex, about being watched, about posing in a sexy way in case someone gets an eyeful. My dad's out of town, doing a story on some elections in Gaspé. No one else is here but me. But probably it's a habit that's hard to break, looking sexy. I wouldn't know.

I only brought one *Seventeen* magazine to read. The magazine's my daydreaming backdrop. I re-read the articles about what I'll need when I start high school: a boy's hair comb to help get rid of dandruff, Noxema and NonOxynol 9 pads for the acne that's sure to sprout, Teen Spirit deodorant for my encroaching woman stink, Playtex tampons for whenever I get my period. I've only had it once so far but it might come again. I figure I'll need to buy all of these items when we get back to the city. I'll do some babysitting, save up some money, and make sure I'm all set for everything adolescent that's going to creep up on me.

When I got my period last December—just as we were on our

way to see *The Nutcracker*—I had to ask Pearl where the maxi-pads were and she said, "Oh, so now that you have your period you think you're a woman?" My father heard. It was embarrassing. I never want to say the word "period" to my father.

I read and re-read the same pages of my magazine, eating the blueberry-jam-smeared toast absently, dropping a bit of black coffee on the pages. Pearl reads the paper like she never does at home. Absorbed. She looks awake, intelligent.

If Pearl speaks to me at the cottage, it will be to talk about the weather. Her voice will be as melodious as a woman in a television advertisement's, but she never looks right at me, never makes eye contact. "It's going to be a perfect day again today," she'll say, turning a page, keeping her face in her paper. Or, "Thundershowers! That'll be good for the flowers!"

I'm trying to be good, I'm trying not to have any fights, so I just answer in my pretend happy teenager voice: "Sounds great! ...Flowers!"

After breakfast I do our dishes and Javex the counters the way Pearl likes it. What you do is you pour a very thin coat of Javex evenly over the counters, maybe a couple of millimetres, let it sit for 10-15 minutes, wipe it all up, then wash them again to make sure there isn't Javex all over the place. It's best to stay on top of chores otherwise I feel overwhelmed and I'll want to procrastinate, which will get me in lots of trouble.

When I'm done I go outside and sit on the porch.

There's a red bird that perches on the fence at the far end of Pearl's jerk mother's property ("Call me Alice!"). Sometimes it's not there, but when it comes by it just sits there on the post, moving its neck and head faster than I can see properly, nervous flicks, one beady black eye spotting me. Spotting me like "I Spy," but also spotting like the way you keep your eye on something when you're doing a fouetté turn in ballet. Like keeping your eye on a smudge on the wall to keep from losing your balance.

I stare at the *Love Story* photo spread in *Seventeen* more than anything else in the magazine. I'm baffled at how the models can get themselves to look the way they do. Matching clothes and shiny hair, genuine happiness sparking in their happy eyes. Where did they find their clothes? How come their schools are so pretty? I put Sun-In on my hair almost every day this summer, but instead of turning blonder it's more orange. I don't know if that's good. Maybe. I am not yet five feet tall, and my hips are growing in but nothing else has yet. Could be I'm going to be huge. It's hard to tell. And I can feel my nose growing. I hope it stops before it turns into my father's nose. He has the family nose: a big, bulbous schnoz.

I stare at the *Love Story* spread—there are six pages of it. I worry about being fat, and then push the worry out of my head. It's like windshield wipers. The worry is the left wiper—it builds up, and the annoyance over the worry is the right—it rubs it out. It isn't the thing to worry about, being fat. Only dumb girls worry about what they look like like that. But I still do, compulsively, almost just to feel the concern itself, a pebble in my belly, a granule of excitement. I worry over it the way you rub a smooth river stone over in your hand, it's hard and warm and present.

Pearl is still inside, listening to her doo-wop music mix. The neighbourhood handyman, Kevin, made a mixtape for her in Montreal. Was she having sex with the handyman while my dad was at work? Was she doing it with Jean-Marie, the Belgian exchange student who rented my bedroom for a month last spring? Was it the potential of doing it with them that aroused her, that made her wear see-through négligées without underpants in the house when they were there? I swallowed my shame to forget my shame that I saw that. She brought the doo-wop mixtape with her everywhere we went, now—in the car, from room to room, from one ghetto blaster to another. Kevin the handyman looked somewhat unhinged, no pun intended. He was lanky and looked hungry and not totally okay. He was often around when I came home from school, hanging out in his one-piece painter man jumpsuit and following Pearl around with his eager googly eyes. I couldn't figure out where we got the money to pay him to do odd jobs when there was never any money for me to get glasses, or new underpants, or school pictures. But it wasn't my habit to voice concerns, so I said nothing about it to my father, or my mother, when I visited her. She wouldn't have cared, anyway. What went on at my father's house was not her affair.

I pull out my journal and make a list of what I've bought with my babysitting money so far, this summer: the magazine, the Sun-In, the biodegradable shampoo. I bought the shampoo for two dollars at a garage sale I went to with my friend Megan. She said you could use biodegradable shampoo to wash your hair in lakes, so I got a grimy little bottle of someone's half-used Lemon Citrus Body Shop. It's gummy but it's still the fanciest shampoo I've ever had.

I grab my biodegradable shampoo and decide to wash in the river. I don't wait for two hours after breakfast; I just go. There's nothing else to do except listen to tapes on my Walkman. I brought six tapes for the whole trip. I'll listen to them on the beach, later, when I'm drying off.

It's still early. Before ten. The birds stopped with that sunrise sound shower they do, and now the sounds they make are more like the river—unexpected, arrhythmic chirps. I wade into the river. The water's knee height for a long time—I can't count how far it is from the shore but it's far. Further than you think. And then you hit the drop. You have to be careful, because the drop is sudden, and deep. As soon as you reach the deep part of the river the water swirls darkly around you. It's almost black, like a potion in a cauldron. It's cold. But it's the best place to swim. I egg-beater my legs while I soap up my hair. I tuck the little tub of shampoo down my suit and push myself underwater to wash the shampoo out. The foam fizzes into the river's currents and is swept away. I open my eyes underwater. You can see a little. Everything is dark green. At least for a few feet, if you look upward. The rest, what's below, is black. I do little half-dives in, up, and under, blowing bubbles from my nose. I float on my back, waving my hands slowly at my sides. I starfish. I flip over and do the Australian crawl: I scissor-kick the way Pearl does when she swims. The prettiest stroke. Something a synchronized swimmer might do. Shoulders almost out of the water, head at a neat angle.

The current is strong. It tugs my body downstream. I know I'm actually moving quickly, but it feels as though I'm drifting in slow motion. A slow-motion dream with ripples of cool and colder waves lapping over and around my body. I keep floating downriver. I've gone too far. I'm not scared. I kick hard with my legs and slice the water with my best crawl—slightly parting my middle and ring fingers the way they taught us in Bronze Medallion—until I'm close enough to spot our cottage. And then I let myself slide along the current again. When I get cold, I cut back in, swimming myself even in the two-foot-deep shallows where I could have waded, then walking on my hands, gripping the sand with my fingers. The sand is full of stones and broken clamshells. It's cold and compact under my palms. I can feel sand filter down my bathing suit.

I collapse on my towel on the beach, landing right on my shampoo bottle. I try to fish it out without moving my bathing suit over any important bits and stand it in the sand beside me. I spray some Sun-In on my hair and lie down on my stomach with my *Seventeen* magazine. I click Chicago into my Walkman. "Will You Still Love Me for the Rest of My Life" is my favourite song. I can imagine how they feel, the people in the song, grown people who love each other. I picture them wearing white button-down shirts and blue jeans and the girl has light brown hair parted on the side and the guy mostly has a nose and a mouth. It makes my stomach queasy, like when I worry about being fat.

I'm good at replaying things. I listen to the song and replay mind-videos of Liam from my ultra dull, super low budget week-long Catholic summer camp. He held my hand when we ran from the gymnasium to the cafeteria in the rain and we used his beach towel as an umbrella. I play the scene over and over. "Will You Still Love Me" and the memory of us running like that. I had never held anyone's hand before. He can make a stone skip five or six or seven times. He can play "Stairway to Heaven" on the guitar, and also "American Pie." But he's too shy to sing loudly. He sort of whisper-sings. *I can't go on, no I can't go on if I'm on my own.* Shhh. I mouth the words.

After a while, I slip on my sandals, shake out my towel, put it around my neck, toss the magazine and the Sun-In and sunscreen into an old straw bag of my mother's and head back up the stony part of the beach to the cottage. I do some chores— clean the bathroom, kind of gross; clean the fridge, definitely gross because of the rotted vegetables in the crisper—then find an old romance novel in the living room and read that for a while. For lunch, I make Pearl and I chicken salad sandwiches, cutting the chicken off the carcass in the fridge. Every time I cut up a chicken I picture gremlins. The bird's ribcage seems malevolent, but the flesh tastes good. I mix it with mayonnaise in a bowl. Cut the sandwiches into triangles. Mix some frozen orange juice and tap water into a container. Set the table with Pearl's braided place mats.

Pearl comes into the dining room and looks at the lunch I laid out. "Thanks, Missy, looks great. You remembered almost everything."

"I forgot to cut some carrots for the side. I'm sorry."

"I don't mind waiting."

❧

My father phones from Cap-aux-Os that night. I'm lying on my cot under the copper crucifix reading *Seventeen* and the romance novel and holy shit the romance novel is a revelation, they are having so much sex, it's so embarrassing. *I can't go on I can't go on I can't go on without you by my side.* I wonder if maybe Liam is thinking about when we ran all the way from the song circle to the gym when it started to rain and we each held part of his towel over our heads.

I can hear my stepmother talking on the phone through the walls. She's saying, "It's hard, you know, doing the single parent thing. You have no idea. I have so much responsibility and there's so much I'd like to do but I'm cooped up here with the kid." She's painting her nails at the same time as she's talking. I can smell the varnish from my room. She has beautiful colours for her toenails. Brownish reds. I want brownish red toenails. I can picture the cotton balls lodged between each of her toes.

I'm not allowed to phone my mother for the month that we're here because that would upset Pearl. Even if I don't live with my mother most of the time, I still miss her. I think about sneaking a call to her but then it would show up on the telephone bill.

I put my headphones back on. *I can't go on I can't go on I can't go on without you by my side*. The batteries are getting old and the wheels are slowing and getting squeaky. I think I got some sand in the battery groove. I say an Our Father and fall asleep with my headphones on, the mothball smell of wool blankets tucked under my chin.

☙❧

After breakfast the next day, Pearl asks if I want to go to the beach with her after I'm done cleaning under the porch.

I say I do.

Cleaning under the porch is disgusting. The top of the porch is crawling with earwigs and they keep falling all over me. I'm not sure if they're really pinching me or if I'm imagining they're pinching me. I run out from under the porch to shake them out of my hair and clothes. The porch is full of rotting old fruit boxes that I pull out and pile up on one side of the property, by an apple tree. We'll bring the boxes to the dump later. I hope we go at sunset, so we can catch black bears rambling and climbing over the heap.

∞

We walk down from Pearl's asshole mother's cottage to the beach. It's bright and hot out. The sun glares down over the river and there's a bit of a mist, so you can't see the other side. You can still make out the little islands that dot the middle of the river. I wish I could live on one of those islands. Surrounded by flat rocks and crooked conifers and the sound of the water rushing around me.

I've brought my shampoo. I walk through the low-level water of the river and swim into the deep part. I egg-beater my legs and pour shampoo over my hair. It's hard to keep my head straight. The water ripples around me and pushes me around even though I beat my legs hard and try to keep myself steady. Some of the shampoo spills into my eye—a big blob of lemony goop. It burns a little but I know it won't last. I count to ten super quick to help the stinging time pass. I lather up my head, move the soap a bit over my body to get the gross feeling of earwigs off me. I tip the little bottle into my swimsuit and dive underwater. When I come up I see the current has pushed me much farther than I thought I'd be.

I can still see Pearl swimming, not that far away. Even from a distance I can tell she's doing her Australian crawl, scissor-kicking strokes beautifully in the water. Crosshatches of sunlight spark off the water.

We never swim the Australian crawl in my swimming lessons, or in the pre-lifeguard prep classes, either. Not speedy enough, I guess, to catch a sinking person. We just do laps and laps and laps of front crawl.

I crawl back to the shore. I split my fingers like I was taught. I kick hard. I get water up my nose and blow bubbles from my mouth. I walk out along the shallows. I drop to my towel.

I watch Pearl from the shore while I flip through my *Seventeen* magazine. Pearl swims the breaststroke, the Australian crawl. She flips onto her back and her arms fly elegantly over her head as she swims backstroke against the rippling river. She goes out deep.

I put on my headphones and push Play. *I can't go on I can't go on . . .*

I think about Liam holding the towel over our heads.

I watch as Pearl's head comes up and goes back down. Her head is so little. Smaller than a pinpoint. An orange prick in the water. She bobs up and down. Her elegant arms, white against the blue grey of the running water, reach up and over. Like a synchronized swimmer. She dives under. She stays underwater so long I get bored of watching.

I turn over onto my stomach. I put my head in my arms. I listen to crows caw to each other. To the wind picking through the pines. To the water flicking and ribboning by, to motorboats in the distance. The sun beats down on my shoulders and back.

I could sleep.

I do.

I fall asleep listening to my Chicago tape. *Will you still love me for the rest of my life I've gotta lot of love and I don't want to let go.*

When I wake, the sun is beginning to set. The sky turns pink over the Ottawa River. It's pretty. The river sounds louder than before. I switch my cassette over to Side B.

I sit up. I look around. No sign of Pearl. I shield my eyes with my right hand, squinting, pretending to be a lifeguard. I stand, walk gingerly to the edge of the water over the hard, rocky sand. I put my hand up to my face again and squint. It reminds me of when I pretended to follow the ball in soccer. Feigning interest. I try it on again and take a good hard look from one end of the horizon to the other.

I slip my sandals on, pull a pair of jean shorts over my bathing suit, shake out my towel and fold it into my straw bag. I walk to the house.

"Hello!" I shout into the cottage. The cottage is dark. No one answers.

I make my way over to the neighbour's house. I knock on the back door. Mrs. Anderson peers out from behind the screen.

"Hi, Mrs. Anderson," I say, "I'm Missy, Pearl's stepdaughter. I can't find Pearl. I don't know where she is."

Mrs. Anderson wipes her hands on the apron around her waist. "Did she go into town?" she asks.

"No, she went for a swim but I don't know where she is now," I say.

"Did you see her go out for a swim?" Mrs. Anderson asks.

"Yes."

"And then what happened?"

"I don't know. I was listening to my tape."

"How long was she out in the water?" Mrs. Anderson opens the screen door. Her eyes scan the horizon. I step out of her way so she can see better. She makes her hand like a lifeguard's too, cupping it over her brow and squinting her eyes at the river.

"I don't know. I wasn't wearing a watch."

"You saw her swimming and then what happened?"

"I fell asleep."

"When did you notice she was missing?"

"I woke up. And I couldn't see her anymore."

"You're very calm!" Mrs. Anderson is not.

"I checked in the house."

"And she wasn't in there, either!"

"No."

"Where's her car?"

"In the driveway."

"You didn't see her in the water? You didn't see if she was struggling?"

"She was diving under the water. I thought she was swimming. She was too far to really see properly."

"You didn't try to call? Or get her?"

"I thought she was having fun. Or washing her hair."

"You didn't do anything?"

"I didn't think I had to."

Mrs. Anderson rushes back into her kitchen. "I'm calling 911," she says. But first she calls the other next-door neighbour. "Jan? Listen, I think there's a problem. There may have been an accident! Pearl's drowned. Or she's missing. Her stepdaughter just wandered in here and—I don't know! She doesn't look nearly upset enough. I'm calling the ambulance! I don't know what to do! Please come over."

I tap Mrs. Anderson on the shoulder. She spins and stares me down, her face red and blotchy, incensed. She's looking at me like I'm crazy.

I say, "Can I borrow your phone? I need to call my mom."

DOWNPOUR

It was pouring. I didn't have an umbrella. My boyfriend Seamus wouldn't have wanted one anyway, he was cheerful about the rain. It reminded him of when he played team sports in autumn storms and skids and falls and rocks under knees hurt with real pain.

Right before the rain came down, the air had the trapped smell of warmed-over cement the day after garbage day. The scythed-out sky glowed a luminous cobalt with the late August transparency of a stained glass window. Then clouds moved over, slow and heavy, and an electrical crackle filled the air. The rain fell hard.

My mother and I used to call big tear-shaped raindrops *des p'tits monsieurs* because they looked like tiny men jumping in and out of puddles. And now I'm getting a memory from when I was about three and my mother had her store and I was in her arms eating a peanut butter and banana sandwich. We looked out at the downpour and she said, *Regarde les p'tits monsieurs*. And I said *p'tits monsieurs*, and her laughter was gentle.

The other story I started—the one from before—happened sometime in the '90s, when I was about twenty. Picture me the way you know me now, except shyer, pudgier, nerdier. I was wearing a Balinese sarong. It was the style of the time. That word, Balinese, reminds me of *baleen*. I definitely thought the whale was my spirit animal, which is why I got the word whale tattooed on my ankle in Chinese characters. So there I was, soaked to my tattooed skin—like, coincidentally, a whale might be. My boyfriend thought I looked hot but I was freezing. Part of the appeal was how visible my nipples were through my bra— padded bras that make breasts look like two scoops of ice cream were not the rage—but it was embarrassing for me, how suddenly exposed my boobs were. My boyfriend said, "Let's go to Westmount Park." And we did, because I was twenty and I didn't speak my mind; it wasn't so far away, and I thought I'd wait in the gazebo while he got his crazy out.

Everyone uses the same shade of greenish grey on benches and stairs and balconies around there—a shabby-chic, rustic, clean, authentic we-got-some-anglo-historical-clout green. The gazebo was exactly that shade of sage green and it was whatever quaint shape—a hexagon or an octagon—and it was fine apart from the teenagers fucking on one of the benches. We ignored each other. They carried on with the carrying on and I hung out like sixteen going down on seventeen was no big deal. The rain was coming down in sheets and there wasn't anyplace else to be. I kept a safe distance, I kept my back to them, wondering how long Seamus would need for his screaming and flinging on the football field.

Too long, turned out. So I traipsed down the freshly painted rain-slicked gazebo steps and back into the storm.

I walked along the field toward Seamus, who was acting like a cat nutted out on catnip. He'd taken off his shirt and kept shouting *more!* at the sky like some fucking urban shaman. My feet slurped in my sandals, and my sandals stuck in the mud. I kicked one right up in the air trying to unstick it, which got me to see the sky again. *Regarde*, my mother says, when she sees clouds like those ones—those tearing kind of cargo-ship-shaped clouds—*regarde comme ils courent. Ils courent!* They ran across the sky, they pushed, they rode, they dumped.

My mother and I used to stand inside the door of the balcony of our apartment just a couple blocks from Westmount Park and watch the rain pour down in summer's big electric storms. She never jumped when the thunder crackled but I did, every time. Drafts slammed doors shut. Bats blew in. And every summer, mid-summer, the rain would turn to hail, and the hail would clatter and crack around us. And that rain smell of cement fizzed and hung around the roads, and everything stopped, abruptly.

By the time I'd waded out to him, Seamus was dangling by his arms from a soccer goal. He'd thrown a rock through the football horns, he said, whatever they're called. I said, "Can we just go now?" He said, "Oh my god you're so hot." He wanted to make out. I was shivering, thinking I was going to get tonsillitis or tuberculosis or pneumonia. He said, "The rain's so warm." I said again, "Can we please just go?" He asked me if I liked the rain—"Don't you like the rain?"—and I told him I liked it better from inside. I knew he was disappointed I was not adventurous. He said it was like dating a *Playboy* centrefold, hot but you can't touch her. "I'm going," I said, and struggled away, in my sandals, through the mud. He got his shirt and jogged up to me. "I didn't think you meant it," he said.

It stopped pouring just as we got out of the park. The sky went clear and starry as if it had never rained. Seamus stopped into a corner store to buy a disposable camera; he snapped a picture of us.

We forgot about the camera. Years later, it turned up in a box after a move. I brought it to a pharmacy and had the photos developed. Most of the pictures were blacked out, but the one Seamus took that night turned out. In the picture, my hair is spiky from the rain. His shirt's soaked through with mud. The sky over Oxford Street takes up most of the shot.

CAROL

He'd lived alone in his small apartment above the diner for the better part of a decade. The smell of grease was generations-soaked into the plaster. The cat litter needed to be cleaned. But all the wood had been freshly polished, and a faint whiff of lemon burst bitter brightness into the air.

Peter sat in his dining chair, long legs crossed, long fingers curled over his knee. He wore baggy corduroys and a tweed jacket that was missing all but one of its buttons. The pants and the jacket sleeves were too short. One sock was white, the other navy silk.

"Dinner's ready!" said Carol. She came out of the little kitchen beside the living room, trailing perfect footprints in foot powder. She looked at him shyly. "Where I used to live, I never got to cook for myself." She put the quiche from the Swiss grocery store on the table and cut it into quarters. Her hand trembled from the weight of the portion on the silver cake knife. "Is this okay?" she asked Peter. "Is this how you do it?"

"That's just fine," Peter answered. "Now why don't you get me a napkin?"

He watched as she jumped into the kitchen, then veered to

the bathroom. Words came through his head: *tickle, delight, amuse, gratify, thrill*. He liked her round, dark eyes and the way her eyebrows furrowed when she was nervous.

"How's this?" Carol asked, holding out a roll of toilet paper, furrowing her brows at him. "I couldn't find any napkins that weren't fancy-pants." She put the toilet paper squarely in the centre of the table and sat down across from him. Her right knee bounced up and down.

"That'll do," said Peter.

Carol unrolled a couple of squares of TP and handed them to him and then took a few for herself. She lit a cigarette. "Cigarettes are harder to quit than heroin, you know."

He thought: *loins, gut, heart. Nostrils*.

"Put it out." He glared at her over his dollar store bifocals. "It reeks."

Carol poised her hand and turned her cigarette into the ashtray beside her plate one, two, three times. Her actions as deliberate and exaggerated as a stage whisper. She would finish her smoke after the frozen chocolate cake. Outside, if that's what he preferred.

"I'm sorry," she said. "Is this what's making you sick? I won't do it again."

"Don't mention it. I may be coming down with something, anyhow. I think a case of rhinorrhea has got me," Peter answered, unrolling squares of toilet paper with which to blow his nose. A trumpeting sound erupted.

"You know what I was thinking about. Elizabeth was in her forties when she had John the Baptist. Post-menopausal babies happen all the time."

Peter filled their glasses with cold white Riesling.

"Of course I can't work, so I'd have lots of time to spend with a baby," said Carol.

He noted her pride with pride. He was glad he could make her happy. It might be good for her, Peter thought. She had never expected to bear children. And she was still young.

"My doctor told me I could," she said.

"It's been a while since I've had a child, as you well know. But with the festival…I'm not sure this would be the time, either. You would have to move in, I suppose."

"My cats don't like to be moved," said Carol. She had four cats. She definitely couldn't move them.

"You know, when I was your age, I was playing all over the world. I tried to discover the organs Bach himself might have played on. I particularly remember southern Germany at this time of the year. And they have a wonderful Bach series in Munich in early March."

❧

When Carol finally left the Douglas she decided to go off her medication. She was grateful for her second chance. She wanted to give back. She thought she had an idea of perfection. You get an idea of perfection in your head and then you go for it even if people say you are nuts, she thought. So she joined the choir at the downtown church with the neon sign. She'd never had any proper training with singing, or anything apart from riding horses, before. But then Peter told her he had a rule he'd stuck by in his twenty-five years of being the church organist, that anyone who wanted to sing could just sing along, and also he, or one of the music students—and they were really just kids, but they were smart kids, doing Masters and PhDs—could certainly afford to spend a little time coaching someone willing to participate in basic music theory.

Carol had come up to him herself, her speaking voice as tremulous as her soprano. Her attention fastened on him. Peter, surprised at the directness of her attention, stammered. "Gar, gar, guh." He faltered, appraising her, and could not speak at all, at first. Her skin was the delicate pink of an albino rabbit. Her hair was auburn, with white roots only slightly apparent at her bangs. She was somewhere about forty, he estimated. Possibly younger. Peter had fiddled with his tie while telling her to help herself to a hymn book, asking if she needed the kind with the music or just the words and if anyone had an extra copy of the response for the coming Sunday. He felt himself blush from close contact with such a young woman. He was wearing a tie with a picture of a cracked egg overflowing with yolk. A favourite of his, chosen by his daughter when she was still in grade school. It always promised attention. This was not the first time a soprano had bent her face in his direction while he was wearing it.

"I might be crazy," Carol had told him when he dropped her off at her apartment, after she'd told him the whole story about the car accident and her brother who'd lied about her being unstable and how they kept her locked up for almost twenty years until her brother died and she was finally free. "I might be crazy but I'm not stupid. I didn't belong there. That place had bad vibes."

"You were misdiagnosed," he'd said. "Our health system is in shambles. A similarly unfortunate incident happened to my neighbour's daughter." His downstairs neighbour's daughter had run away into the streets in her nightgown one autumn afternoon. No one could find her, not even the police. She turned up in Edmundston, New Brunswick, still in her pyjamas, a week later.

He wished that everyone would have higher standards. And pride in their work. If they felt proud they would be happy to be good doctors and then people would get better treatment. People like Carol and his downstairs neighbour's daughter wouldn't have wasted almost entire lifetimes because of a single professional's utter incompetency.

❧

"What do you remember about your life from before that time?" Peter asked Carol. He liked to hear her stories about her childhood on the Prairies.

"I remember riding horses at my uncle Hal's farm in Saskatchewan," said Carol. She scooped up pieces of her quiche with a teaspoon. Quiche was sort of like flan, she thought. And it was nice to eat it as if it was a dessert. "I lived there off and on from the time I was four until I was about seventeen. I liked going to dances, too," she said, smiling at the memory.

She glanced at her waiting, half-smoked cigarette and chewed on a hangnail. Her nails were bitten past the quick. She licked her torn skin over-delicately, knowing she was being watched, the way a cat preens her face, rough tongue over fur.

Peter smiled at her with his eyes.

"Did I ever tell you about the time I fell off a horse?"

"I don't think you did, no."

"Well my brother said I fell off a horse, once, and that it

stepped on my head, but I don't have a scar on my head so I don't believe him. Horses are extremely heavy and I would have felt it for sure. It would have left a horseshoe print on me, which could have been lucky. If it wasn't so unlucky a thing to happen, to have a horse step on you."

"That would most certainly have been unlucky," said Peter, reaching for her hand.

Carol patted his hand, then withdrew hers. She stood up, collected the plates, and carried the dishes into the kitchen. "Do you want dessert now or just skip it?" she called.

"Let's just skip it," he said.

It wasn't that Peter was unaware of the way Carol's ass moved. It was an adorably squishy sort of ass. But it was her brand new fresh-hatched exuberance that made him turn his head, and wave a little when she turned and smiled at him broadly, and broader still, wider than a mouth should go.

❧

"There's something here," Carol told Peter. "I can feel a presence."

"Stop worrying yourself. Go back to sleep." He adjusted his red tuque and rolled away from her.

Carol slid back into her flowered nightgown and stepped onto the threadbare hooked rug Peter's late wife had designed. She pushed her hair off her face and listened. She took the striped blanket off the bed and with her into the living room, remembering her friend Robin at the hospital who had told her about talking to ghosts. The ticking clock above the door read three. Carol shuffled to the record player. Its arm reached over and found a groove in the vinyl where it rested. Music shifted out from the speakers. Carol didn't know the tune. She read the name on the disk as it spun. Pur-Pur-Purcell.

Carol knelt by the stereo. The music was tender, like church music. She wrapped the woollen blanket more tightly around her body. Leaned her head against the Victorian table legs and closed her eyes.

❧

Peter found Carol in the morning when he got up to make himself a cup of tea. Blanket wrapped around her shoulders, her whitewash face backlit by the dark light of the wintry morning. Frozen branches scraped against the living room windows. Beyond, a frozen Birnam, a forest of icicles glazing the park across the boulevard.

How did he get so lucky, he wondered.

"Wake up, woman," he said. "It's morning."

LANDSLIDE

I can't remember how I heard about the party. It was in an upper duplex. Someone had invited me, a friend of a friend of a roommate who said they'd meet me but never showed.

By the time I arrived the place was packed. I crammed myself into the hall, fighting a natural inclination for solitude and a panicky desire to escape. The air was more humid exhalation and body odour than air.

A band was playing in the front part of the double living room across the hall, but the room was filled to capacity and I couldn't make out who the band was, if I would have even known. I pushed my way through the crowd saying "thank you" instead of "sorry" to get people to shift out of the way, and I stepped out onto the rickety, slanting front balcony to hear the band play through the window. There were a few people out there already, and the porch strained beneath our weight. I thought of my friend Dimitra, whose balcony, just a few roads over, had collapsed onto the street the previous spring after a thaw. I decided this one would hold up at least while I considered my game plan. I lit a cigarette and debated whether or not to leave.

The city's humid heat wrapped around us like gauzy net. Everyone, both outside on the balcony and inside the apartment, was covered in a fine sheen of sweat. It beaded over the hair of our sunburnt arms, over our upper lips, along our cheeks. Crickets whirred mechanically en masse. It was rare to hear them so loud in the city.

The strains of a plunky, out-of-tune upright piano played, and I caught, through the frame of the front window, the vigorous arm motions of a woman strumming strings from a broom in a bucket. I could hear a mandolin. A cello. The energy of the music and the new moon heat of the night combined to fill the summer air with an ephemeral sense of possibility. I decided to stay.

I pushed my way back inside the apartment, my arms sliding against others, down the hall, and into the kitchen, where the crowd was thinner. The fire escape door was open and a breeze drifted in. Beers bobbed in a cooler of melted ice by the fridge. I grabbed one. The bottle was wet but still relatively cool. I put it against my forehead for a moment, then tucked my hand into the bottom of my skirt to twist off the cap. I couldn't see a garbage bin so I put the cap into my purse.

A woman with waist-length hair sat cross-legged on a broken armchair, regaling a group of women. She was small, I guessed just under five feet, and lithe. Her hair, frizzy from the humidity, fanned out around her tiny body like a veil. She wore a green cotton dress with spaghetti straps. You could see the shape of her breasts through the material and it was both natural and provocative. She was talking about the professors from her art school who'd paid her for sex. Describing how she'd had a driver who would escort her to her john, a shop teacher from the school she'd gone to. How he fucked her up the ass and then she shat out worms.

I wondered whether that was even possible, shitting out worms from sex. What the fuck was the shop teacher up to. I wondered if it was the dad of the two girls I used to babysit—Nadine and Marie-Jade. I remember him telling me he taught shop or sculpture or something to do with saws at the downtown college. He'd seemed so gangly and awkward; it was hard to imagine him hiring this woman for sex and giving her butt worm diseases.

It felt voyeuristic to stand there, listening to someone I didn't know talk about such intimate things. But she was compelling. I didn't want to go anywhere else. I lifted my arms to feel the breeze move under them and shifted my legs so that a little air from the fire escape could move under my skirt and cool the backs of my knees. I drank from the beer in big gulps.

The band was still playing. Jive-y, thumpy, old-timey music, fancy cello arpeggios in counterpoint, the oompa-pa of the piano keeping tempo. A man with a ragged voice sang but the instruments drowned out his words.

The woman on the chair went on with her story. She said after the worms she'd decided to get a real job, so now she worked as a character illustrator for a gaming company. Her dad had paid for her to go back to a ten-month digital art program but first she'd had to go to rehab. Because, by the way, she'd been on heroin, she laughed. She'd forgotten to tell that part of the story before. She took a swig of her beer.

I took another swig of mine.

The woman switched topics abruptly and started talking about how she liked to taxidermy dead squirrels she found on the side of the road in the city. She pulled all her hair from around her and tied it in a knot over her head as she spoke. She didn't seem to be wearing any makeup. The knot slid over and cast a shadow over her cheekbones. A fascinator built of hair.

She was talking about the dead squirrels in her freezer and how her roommate didn't like them but she wanted to do a whole tableau of them—like a happy dead squirrel family in her living room. She was even knitting outfits for them all and making them real felt hats with a tiny little hat stand she'd fashioned out of one of those little jointed wooden dolls art students use to learn to draw human proportions accurately. She was going to position the squirrels, once they were all stuffed, into stilled moments of activity: cooking, dancing, reading, and so on. And the shop teacher—they were friends now, it was cool—was building a kind of dollhouse for the squirrels to live in more permanently.

I didn't remember ever encountering a dead squirrel. Maybe I didn't know where to look for them. I'd seen some dead animals on highways but they were mostly cats or groundhogs or porcupines, skunks or raccoons. I couldn't remember ever seeing a single dead squirrel in all my life.

"I've never seen a dead squirrel," I offered.

At first she barely acknowledged I'd spoken, pausing only slightly before continuing to say that her freezer was full of dead animals, then, extending eye contact, including me in her queenly way, she added that sometimes they had worms.

I remained rapt in the crowd of listeners. The folk band pounded beats from the front of the house while the woman on the chair kept up with her gross-out yarns.

I was thirsty. I finished my first beer and then grabbed another, adding the second cap to my purse.

Phoenix, she told me her name, it was Phoenix, unfolded her legs from her perch. "What kind of beer is that?" she asked me.

"Just a Bud."

She reached into the cooler and grabbed herself one. "Wanna see if there's any merch?"

We made our way to the front of the apartment. The crowd had thinned a little. We joked around while we looked at the burned CDs and Xeroxed liner notes. It turned out the band was from Truro, Nova Scotia. The tall singer, who also played trombone, said hi to Phoenix. They knew each other from tree planting in Manitoba. "This guy was a total pro," she told me, poking the singer in the chest. "He even flew helicopters!"

"Cool!" I said.

"I went in helicopters sometimes," the singer said. "To figure out where the saplings had been cached. I didn't fly them."

A woman came up behind him and tucked herself under his arm.

"Ah," Phoenix whispered to me. "The Chosen One. Every time I wonder who it will be," she said.

I told Phoenix I was curious about her taxidermy. She said she'd show me her squirrels and she wrote down her phone number on my cigarette pack. "Wait," she said to me, "what's your name?"

"Agnes."

I realized I was holding a CD and that the singer and the Chosen One were looking at me expectantly, so I forked over my cab money, slid the CD into my purse. We all kiss-kissed goodbye. I went down the stairs and out onto the street. Walked the forty-five minutes northwards back to where I lived. It felt like I was swimming home in tepid bathwater under a grinning moon.

We met up the next week. I was supposed to go to Phoenix's place to see the squirrels but I'd told her I'd just gotten a new job at a commercial gallery in the Old Port and she wanted to go out to celebrate that instead. We went to a bar I'd frequented as a teenager. It was just as packed with underage drinkers as it used to be except they looked richer—they all wore popped collars and easy life expressions. We sat in the front to watch the passersby from the ledge of the window against which we both leaned an elbow. She was wearing high-waisted jeans with a man's T-shirt tucked into them. Her hair was braided over her head like a crown. I had a picture of my grandmother with her hair like that.

I felt like a normcore blob. Teen store jeans. Tank. Same old cheap Chinese shoes. I had good earrings on, though. Vintage red enamel.

I ordered what I used to get—a pitcher of red. The waitress came back with the plastic jug and two cold steins. "I'm sober," Phoenix said, "but I can still drink." I didn't know if I was enabling her or if this was normal. I poured myself a beer and let her decide. She poured herself a beer that was half head and drank from it immediately, not minding the foam.

Phoenix had a hickey on her neck, sort of towards the front. It was distracting. I'd look at her all composed and normal and then glance at the hickey again. Wondering if it would taste woundish, like a canker sore inside your mouth.

Phoenix said, "You should come to this thing I'm going to on the weekend. It's a really cool personal growth seminar. It can help make your life better, like help you do better at your job, like sell more paintings, stuff like that."

She looked me right in the eyes. Her sense of hope made me

doubt my doubts. I'd had some reservations about the truth of her worm stories.

" "What is it?" I asked. I started to fold my cardboard coaster in at the corners.

"It's just like a few seminars to help get you better at your job or be on top of things. My dad got me into it. It's like that book *The Secret*. I know it sounds cheesy but it's about changing your outlook on life and taking responsibility for your mistakes. It's called Landslide. It's a worldwide thing. It's got programs in over twenty countries around the world." Phoenix looked out at the street and had a drink and said, "It's been really good for me."

"That's great," I said. "Did you know you can only fold any piece of paper eight times? Apparently?" I showed her my folded up coaster.

"It's made me closer to my family. After the seminar, I apologized for a lot of stuff I did. I really owned all my shit for the first time in a long time, you know."

"Sounds intense. Maybe I can make my mom go."

She sized me up, then shifted her glance back outside. "Yeah, well, maybe it's not your jam."

"Okay, now I feel bad," I said. "I didn't mean to be rude. What do you like about it?" I put the folded coaster aside. It wouldn't stay flat. I had to keep my thumb on it. I looked at Phoenix.

"It's like you learn how an event just happens to you and it's not positive or negative. It just something that happens. Then how you interpret it is what they call 'a sea of responses.' Good or bad interpretations. It's how you tell yourself the story of what happened to you. You know?"

"So, like, it's about reframing how you think about what happens to you?"

"Yeah, it's changing your story. It's really powerful."

It was late but people were still milling with activity along the street, which was closed to traffic for a street festival. We drank in silence, watching the crowds as they meandered up and down the road like flocks of birds, converging, breaking up, swarming, winnowing. The dumpling seller song-called for two-dollar Styrofoam platters of dumplings in peanut sauce. Someone was selling a table-full of orange thongs across the road. A scrappy clown juggled bowling pins she'd lit on fire.

"Ever been to clown school?" I asked.

"No. I did rhythmic gymnastics for a while."

"The one with the ribbons."

"Yeah. Listen, I'm sorry. It's been so long since I was on a date with a girl. I don't really know how to act."

My stomach lurched. "I didn't think this was a date," I said. Was it a date? "I don't usually...I date guys?"

"Oh, wow. Oh, okay."

"Awk-ward..." I said.

We looked at each other, laughed, and cheersed our steins.

"Anyway, I like your hair. My grandma used to do her hair like that."

She smiled and touched her braid. "It's not that hard to do," she said. "So, how come you got into art?"

"I don't know. I always liked drawing. I've worked in commercial galleries for a while. It's a nice way to earn money. I could never just be an artist. I'm probably not good enough."

"What do your parents think?"

"My parents don't really get it."

"Did they expect you to be a dentist or something?"

I'd always felt that dentistry would be a particularly revolting field to work in. All those strangers' hanging-open mouths full of rot. "No. There was never that kind of expectation for me. More like just stay out of prison and don't get knocked up."

The waitress came back and we ordered another pitcher. I paid, in case it was a date.

"So, those stories you were telling at the party were pretty heavy."

"Yeah, that was fucked. I shouldn't talk so much."

"How did all that start? Can I ask?" I half-asked because I wanted to see if it was really real.

"A few years ago I was super broke. My family wouldn't help me out anymore because they knew I was using. I'd just moved from Vancouver and I don't speak French. I was having a hard time finding any job. And like, I was using, so, that was expensive. I was checking ads on Craigslist. It started because I got a sugar daddy on Craigslist, honestly."

"I've heard about that."

"Never done it?"

"No."

"I didn't think I'd go through with it. That first guy sent me his picture. He looked like a ginger Peewee Herman. He had red hair and a gross puffy nose. Huge nostrils. It was a thousand bucks a month for one visit a week. It helped me pay my bills."

"Must have been tough."

"Sometimes it was fine. Sometimes it was brutal. Sometimes it was just boring."

I wondered if I'd ever be able to go through with something like that. I've had some one-night stands. It might not be so different. I wondered what the old lady version of myself would think of it. Would she think, looking back, that I had had chutzpah or that I'd ruined myself?

"So what do you think about coming with me to Landslide?"

"I'm not sure it's for me," I said. "Is that okay?"

Cops in fluorescent yellow vests arrived and moved the barricades on the street. After a while regular traffic resumed, pedestrians teetered into cabs.

"Do you want to walk?" I asked.

We left the bar and walked up Saint-Laurent towards Little Italy.

We stopped and sat down at a park in front of an old church turned condo building and watched groups as they spilled sloppily out of brasseries and bars and Italian restos.

The bench was broken right under my thighs and it pricked them. Phoenix played with a piece of wood. I picked up a little branch from the ground and tore at the bark. It was still warm out, but not the same heat-wave hot as the night of the party.

The cars to our left moved north. To our right they moved south. A couple kids whizzed by on skateboards. I imagined who Phoenix would date. Someone with a guerrilla garden. Someone who composted. I invented a list of stereotypes to make myself feel better.

"I'm feeling stressed right now," Phoenix said. "I hate feeling stressed." Her face was generous in its vulnerability, its lack of makeup. Vital. Present.

"Okay. So let's call it a night," I said.

I kissed each of her cheeks.

"Bye!" she called.

I walked off with my hands in my pants pockets, shuffling in

my old Chinese shoes, my stomach exploding with a despair
that surprised me. I knew from experience it would begin to feel
like lightness after a while.

Grief the breath in.

Relief the breath out.

THE INTRUSION

The tattooed man clambered up the fire escape to the top storey. He hoisted open the guillotine window and stepped into the room. His friend, Ti-Guy, also known as Ti-Pit, lagged behind as always. Those tiny knees couldn't muster their old strength ever since that last bad fall. The tattooed man shouldered against the window; his friend crept in by the radiator.

"You in? You all right?" asked the tattooed man.

"Yeah, yeah," answered Ti-Pit. They looked around. They were in a room furnished with an open suitcase, a paper lamp, and a cot.

The girl on the cot wasn't asleep. She looked at the men through half-closed eyes. Like a prayer card picture of a saint, a choir of porcelain dolls arced over her head. The dolls stared down the intruders more openly than the girl.

"What are you doing here?"

The tattooed man thought it was one of the dolls talking, and started, but it was the blonde girl. "*Tabarnak,*" whispered Ti-Pit. "She's awake!"

The girl opened her eyes. In the dark the tattooed man could make out only two black indentations. As if her eyeballs had been plucked out.

The girl had half-expected someone to climb into her window one night. But she'd thought that it would be some sort of urban destiny boy who'd see her and they'd love each other and get married when they woke up as adults. She imagined this would happen all of a sudden. She'd wake up with breasts, too big for any of her little girl clothes, needing lacy underwear, needing tampons. Instead, she got these two men in coveralls and her legs still didn't make it even three-quarters of the way down the mattress.

There was a rustling sound as one of the dolls, the life-sized one, moved protectively close to the girl. The girl said, from a hole in her face, "What are you guys doing here, anyway?"

"Well," answered the tattooed man, squatting beside the bed, a safe distance from the dolls. "Well, we were going to rob this apartment, see, but we got the wrong building, I think." The girl liked the tattoo of the stallion on his shoulder even though it was cut in half by the strap of his overalls.

"Yeah," whispered Ti-Pit, still hunched against the radiator, "yeah, we got the wrong house, that's for damn sure!"

The girl's doll sat up straight and put her hand over her mouth. "Oh no! The wrong house!" The tattooed man couldn't make out if the doll's lips had really moved.

The girl got out one of those pretend bottles, the kind that make liquid seem as though it's being drunk. She fed it to the doll beside her. "Here, Flora. You must be really thirsty."

Flora the doll said, "I can do it!" And she took the bottle herself.

"My mother will be very sad if you rob us because we hardly have anything," the girl said, keeping her eyes fixed on her doll.

The tattooed man felt gargantuan, as if he'd grown ten feet.

The porcelain bodies of the dolls slowly stood up on the bed and walked rigidly toward the men, climbing over the girl's legs until the little choir, no, the little army of dollies stood between the men and the girl. Colonies of pigeons cooed on the windowsills of the apartments. The moon hung just over the roof of the next building.

"Sorry, like we said, we got the wrong house!" said Ti-Pit.

The doll with the bottle waved bye-bye with one hand while she continued to drink. The other dolls watched the men. Then their glass eyes slid back and they blinked, the patchy hair of their eyelashes brushing their cheeks momentarily before snapping open again and staring ahead. The tattooed man pushed out through the window and grabbed Ti-Pit by the arm to haul him out. He piggybacked Ti-Pit down the fire escape. Once in the alley, the tattooed man dropped him and they made a run for it, each man for himself.

The little girl fell fast asleep.

In the morning, she said to her mother, "*Maman*, there were men in my room last night, but they said they had the wrong apartment, so they left."

"That's not a nice dream, dear. Finish your cereal, please."

When the girl had eaten her breakfast she went back to her room, where she found her dolls had made the bed, then laid their bodies down tidily over the white coverlet. Their eyes closed, they looked peaceful, like a lineup of dead babies at a wake.

PARC LAFONTAINE

Serge told Louise ever since his book was published, women kept assuming he wanted to give it to them up the ass. "You know what they say," she said, "about making an ass out of you and me." But he wasn't listening. He said he'd pick up whatever girl at whatever foosball bar on Mont-Royal and get her back to his place, you know: slam the door with your hip, *ma belle*, and mind the recycle bins in the hall. Then there'd be some gin and tonics and some sofa and some clothes off and she'd turn, and he'd grudgingly give it to her like that scene in the book, at the end. He said that part wasn't even true, or maybe it was true, but he didn't even like it that much, he just felt like he had to do it. They'd switched to talking in French, and in French up the ass has its own word, a verb—like bugger, except people still actually say it. *Enculer*.

They were sitting at the top of the stands at Parc Lafontaine watching a game of *pétanque*. Four o'clock sunlight burned Louise's shoulder blades—"I'm so white I can burn even in nighttime," she said. The 45 rattled up Papineau. A lawnmower whined. The *pétanque* was getting heated. A man with a couple of strands of greasy hair cussed out a skinny, gap-toothed woman for losing a ball somewhere beyond the tennis courts. She was Hochelaga-poor skinny, underfed-from-infancy skinny. The whole team had halfway house faces.

Serge pulled his bag onto his lap. It was a French-from-France brand with a changing mat and a little stuffed animal hanging off a chain. He pulled the mat out to show Louise. "This is for when you want to read in the park," he said. He didn't know it was a diaper bag.

He said, "I stopped seeing the other girls."

He said, "Why are you seeing that Venezuelan? Don't meet up with him. Come over to my place."

Louise said, "This is the fucking Bukowski Lawn Bowling League."

Serge laughed to feel like he could laugh. Like he wanted to like her enough to laugh with her again.

Serge said, "Is the Venezuelan prettier than me?"

She said, "He's pretty."

❧

After Serge left, Diego met her at the park. Some wannabe played the theme to *Close Encounters* on his flute. People were still lying around half-naked on *Patates Frites* Hill, looking like oily fries stuck to the grass. In a good way. In a seeing-people-half-naked-outside way. Even the man cooling his Speedoed half-erection and full *bédaine* in the green light of dusk.

Diego told Louise about his gig with the circus, how he'd played a lute with wings pinned to his back while acrobats swam in a pool of real chocolate. Diego's face was cherubic, brown. He smelled like strawberry ice cream. He put his *mochila*, his straw bag, under their heads, and they lay in the grass and held hands, watching the motion of the leaves, listening to squirrels shimmy along the branches.

LEG UP

I was by myself in the apartment. I stood in front of the hallway mirror. I was practicing.

I stood with my right leg bent behind me, under my kilt, and imagined myself to have only the one leg, the left—and the stump, the right. Standing that way, I could see my kneecap rounding out from under the hem of my uniform. A knob of Band-Aid beige flesh.

I talked to the hallway mirror. More often than I should. I practiced what I would say in different circumstances. Like how to talk to Deborah, whose locker was beside mine, or how to get Sami, the guy from band who played bass clarinet and took the same bus home as me, to ask me out. Later, as I heard myself speak the rehearsed phrases aloud, and listened to the locker girl and the band guy repeat the phrases I had invented for them, actually say what I'd expected and practiced they would, it seemed as though my entire world sprouted from my invention, and I grew bored with it, and sabotaged things to see what would happen when we went off-script. And then people would look at me with their eyes large and hurt. As if they knew I'd said the wrong thing, taken the words they were scripted to speak from them and left them without recourse.

I stood in front of the hall mirror every day before school and wondered what I would look like with only a half leg on the right. I'd recently read a YA book where a girl gets bone cancer in her leg and needs it amputated. She is fine, afterwards, but it is hard for her and her family for about a year while they adapt.

I dreamed, after reading the book, that that had happened to me. I dreamed I'd been diagnosed with a terrible, advanced-beyond-treatment cancer and I had to break the news to my parents. They cried. I'd also recently dreamed of a man sawing off his own leg on the side of the road to Gaspé and it felt like a premonition. It felt like I was rehearsing, in my dreams, the way I have in the mirror.

The first doctor, our family doctor, Dr. Devé, who I asked about hypothetical potential development for my ideal leg, got an almost cartoony look of shock and disgust on his old little psoriasis-scaly red-and-white face and, his hand trembling, referred me to a psychiatrist. I didn't tell my parents. I crunched his scrawled reference up inside my coat pocket and told my mom everything was fine, super breezy.

But I affected a bit of a limp on the way home. I thought of the limp as the breaking-in process.

The thing about a bowl of icing sugar is this. You lick the spoon and push it against the powdered sugar and then it sticks to your mouth. That sticking part is addictive. I always want to feel it again as soon as I've swallowed it. I like to eat bowls of powdered sugar sometimes, when my mother's asleep and the dog is asleep and only the cat watches me. I let her sit on the table when my mom's not looking. We blink at each other.

The other night, after eating a bowlful of powdered sugar, I bound my leg up for the first time with an embroidered Mexican belt that was more like a flat rope. I wrapped it in crisscrosses. It looked pretty. I had to sleep on my side because sleeping on my back didn't work with my leg like that—it made me arch my back too much and it hurt a lot more than I thought it would.

In the morning I dropped my nightgown over my bound-up leg and hopped into the kitchen.

The dog was asleep on her yellow beanbag pillow by the sliding doors.

"Morning," said my mom.

"Morning," I said, hopping to the fridge.

"Only a bit of juice left," Mom said.

"Okay," I said, and poured what little was left into the bottom of a Duralex glass. "The law is hard but it is the law," is what Duralex means. In Greek? In Latin probably. I hopped to the dining room and sat on my good side, leaning the bound-up leg away from me.

My mouth tasted like fungus from not having brushed my teeth after the powdered sugar. The orange juice didn't help as much as I wanted it to. I thought it might be like an acid treatment, a super scrub of the mouth. But it was just juice taste on top of fungus taste.

"You all right?" Mom asked.

"Yup," I said, pouring my cereal, standing in my cloud of bad breath. I breathed in and out and in and out. "All good."

The counter between us hid my hidden leg.

"Do you have any tests today?" my mother asked.

"Calculus," I told her.

"I never had to do calculus at school," she said.

"I know," I said, and hopped back to my room. The orange juice slopped onto my nightgown. It made me happy. Proof, I thought, rubbing at it. Proof of intention. Proof of a successful hop. Proof.

In the old days, before anaesthetic, people who were injured in wars, on ships, in mills, they had to have their limbs amputated while they were awake. They had to be aware of the sawing. Sometimes the doctors would give them a swig of alcohol straight from a stubby brown bottle. And then they'd give them a chunk of leather or a switch of kindling to chew on. The patient would chomp their teeth down as hard as they could to bear the idea and the pain of being sawed to pieces. Maybe the thing in their mouths was also to keep them from screaming, from distracting the doctor. Sometimes barbers acted as surgeons, in olden times. I guess because they had the sharp tools already, the clean floors. What would a limb sound like as it fell to the floor? Bonk. Probably a kind of bonk. The dripping of blood would sound like water. Or ketchup. Splurty.

There are very few people in the world who've had to saw off their own limbs. The hiking guy who got stuck in a canyon, maybe some other people in extreme circumstances. The thing is even if you feel you are meant to live life without a limb the doctors won't do it. Even if you tell them about how you'd rather live they don't care, they have their oath that they make when they graduate medical school, about doing no harm. And they think you're crazy. I read about it online. When people like me come up to them with our half-leg suggestions, the doctors say, "I won't harm a perfectly healthy body." It's good enough for some people, that kind of answer. Some people are probably like, Sure okay, you're right, I'm healthy and just being a little goofy about not wanting my leg. I guess I'll just keep it now. I have different standards.

I sat on the edge of my bed and unbound my leg. The criss-crosses of the belt looked like welts. There were deep ridges along my thigh and my shin felt tender. I stretched out my leg and tested my weight on it. Every tiny movement hurt. Hurt like maybe I'd bruised the bone. If it could be a colour the pain would be purple. Blackish purple. It definitely felt weaker. It tingled and ached from having been stuck like that for so many hours while I slept. I dressed and limped out of my room. A genuine limp. Progress.

The calculus test was easy. Our entire grade had to take it in the auditorium. I had to pee the whole time. My leg had its own rhythm. I thought pulse. I thought pulsar. I thought pulp.

After the exam, I went to the cafeteria and bought my lunch. I got all gross things I don't like. A hamburger, an ice cream sandwich, a cup of slimy sweet fruit. I ate every bit. A prefect told me to tuck in my shirt, so I did, in my mind's eye giving them the double bird as they rounded the hall. I hate prefects. I hate their burgundy cardigans and their A+ attitudes. It's not about actual grades. It's about a certain gradient of affected and grating morality.

No one talked to me. I limped over to the library and read *Gone with the Wind*. And then I went home.

I told my mother I got home early because it was exam period.

The school had called, though, so she knew I'd skipped classes to hang out at the library again. I didn't think they'd do that because of being so busy with exams. Oh well.

I was sitting in my bed, one leg in front of me, the other bent at the knee, blankets over me, reading *Gone with the Wind*.

Mom said, "Honey, what's going on? Your behaviour is a bit

unusual these days. The hopping around. The skipping school. Is this something I need to worry about?"

I wished I could tell her about the rush of happiness I feel when I reimagine my life without my shin and foot.

"Do you have enough light to read?" she asked. "How can you be comfortable sitting like that?" she asked. She came in and turned on my bedside light, and the light over my desk.

"I'm okay," I said. "I like it like this."

"Are you sick? Do I need to call the doctor?" she asked. She brushed my bangs aside and felt my forehead.

"Maybe," I said. "I think I aced my math test."

"You always do," she said, looking at me with her extra sensor eyes trying to read me. I slacked the muscles of my face and made my face blank as a sheet, blank as printer paper.

"What on Earth is going on in that noggin?" she asked me, pretending to knock on my head. Knock, knock, knock. "I can't read you anymore." She looked sad. The little lines around her mouth deepened. Her chin got a dimply orange rind look to it.

"Don't worry, Mom," I said. "I'm just trying to figure out who I want to be."

A teen line; a bone to chew on.

"Sure," she said.

She kept looking at me with her eyebrows up, her tentacle eyes boring into me, trying to grab my secret out of my head.

"Have you ever heard of people missing a leg?" I broached, casually.

"I've heard of that," she said.

She said, "I remember when you started to walk, your beautiful little legs were so strong. Your little feet were so straight. You walked sooner than any other baby I knew."

She said, "Hey, do you want to look at pictures of when you were a baby with me? Please?"

She was cute in her nostalgic mommy mode so I said okay.

She came to sit beside me in the bed, and together we flipped through the album of the first year of my life. I saw pictures of myself pointy-headed and alien at birth in my mother's tired, happy arms. I saw myself as a toddler, curly-haired and laughing in the grass beside the neighbour's orange cat, my little fat legs in unworn crisscross leather sandals pointing right out towards the camera.

"See how beautiful you are?" my mother said. "You're sixteen months old in this picture. I never thought I would have a baby at my age," she said. "My little miracle. When you were born I said to myself, she's new life come into an old world."

She didn't look at me when she said that. She kept looking at the album but she didn't turn the page, and I saw she wiped at her eye with the back of her palm. My grandma used to say my mother had "the gift of tears," which just means she cries at commercials and when she looks at baby pictures. But it's a nice thing about her.

THE KNOCKOFF ECLIPSE

The dress blushed. Henry felt abashed. He wasn't used to public displays of affection. Fibre optic letters latticed the rim of the girl's dress, scrolling its hem in a double retro shadow of old school datatext crossed with needlepoint: HOT HOT HOT HOT worked its bright way against her bare knees. The dress went dark before a valentine heart blossomed against her chest. The heart split and reformed, pumping pink-blue-red to the remastered rhythm of The Police's "Every Breath You Take." Henry pulled at the neck of his plaid shirt. He felt out of place. He turned his back on the girl in the dress. Probably the ebullient signage wasn't intended for him. The barmaid moved toward him, glowing headband haloing her face in the tangerine softness of a Rembrandt.

"What can I get you?" she asked.

"I'll just have a beer. Whatever."

"Pint?"

"Pint." He took a bill out of his front pocket.

"I think the lady there likes you," she said.

"Maybe."

In his late teens Henry had been in a cover band and he'd played a few gigs here, when the place had been more of a dive.

He liked it better before all this after-school tube-top bouncing. In the old days he'd get hosed every show and scream his lungs out and girls would buy him pitchers of Molson and shots of Jäger and touch his hair. It went to his shoulders then, and he'd tell people to call the colour "gold," not blonde or red, and women would ask if it was his natural colour and he'd say yeah, and he'd have his pick of which one to bring home. He preferred the chubby ones. They were sweeter at first. Less subject to cattiness, menstrual crying, badgering.

Henry glanced over his shoulder at the girl with the dress. She was still there, lit up in the clichéd shades of a Miami sunset. The whole place flickered with glowing garments; bodies roved like constellations, their clothes blinking off and on from dark corners of the bar. The room heated to nauseating from their mass. They were like fireflies, if this was summer, if this was Lake Memphremagog in the summertime where his parents had a place where he caught fireflies in jars made just for that.

Henry felt motion-sick. He looked again. The girl took a swig from her glass. It was hard to see what she looked like behind the blinking dress. He watched the head of his beer fizz in the dim. He was not lit.

Poof. She was beside him. Snuck up with her lights off. Flipped them back on to a medium glow; she was the lampshade to his chesterfield.

"So what, you're illiterate?" Her face was underlit porcelain symmetry.

He could see up her almost-identical nostrils. She looked like a kid trying to spook someone out at a campfire, her chin making a big shaded V up her face. She blinked and the shadows on her eyelids blinked. Her lashes and the stubble that pricked along her scalp were red. She appeared not to have eyebrows. She stood there, mock accusatory in her lustrous, breathing getup. He wasn't drunk enough for this to be effortless. "I can read. But what would I say in these duds?"

"I could bedazzle them for you." She had a false-deep, quasi-puppetty voice. Like when someone makes a joke and it bombs and there's a goosey synth *wah wah*.

"You good with wires?"

"Well, I made this." She twirled to show him her confection, tipsy, self-conscious and proud, blurring like a long-exposure photograph. The dress reacted to her movement and fluttered in slow motion, mocking Marilyn's moment and spotlighting her bare legs for his viewing pleasure. Nothing like watching a woman twirl. He felt bedazzled already.

"Are you gonna tell me your name, or does your dress do that for you too?" Henry asked.

Her dress could do that for her too. It spelled out each letter of her name in a necklace of imitation Scrabble tiles: W-A-N-D-A. Then WANDA WANDA WANDA WANDA ringed and stamped across her chest and around her waist in different sizes and fonts.

"Nice to meet you, Wanda," said Henry. "I'm Henry." He held out his hand, like people used to do before they'd programmed their clothes to talk for them.

Henry asked the haloed barmaid for another round. Wanda plunked down some cash of her own for a pack of triple As, which she plugged into a pocket by her hip.

"Where you from?" she asked.

"Up North."

"Like Laval?"

"Like all the way up North."

"Oh, like with the dams."

"Yeah."

"You been here before?"

"When they had a pool table."

"In the epoch of the cheap drink."

And so on. Her dress purring, and a kitten on the dress turning into a fish that pulsated quietly at her belly button. The smell of beer and the smell of gin and the smell of sweat heavy in the room.

Skip to after a while, when the 1980s-era anthem chords were getting to him, and Henry told Wanda it couldn't possibly be safe for her to walk home alone in times likes these, and she agreed. She followed him to the coat check. She didn't need a jacket. She'd just turn her beams on high.

They walked up blacked-out Saint-Laurent and then over to Saint-Dominique, Wanda's dress casting conical illuminations over the snowed-over streets. "Good thing you've got that dress or we wouldn't see too much," said Henry, and Wanda said, "Yeah." Only a few tanks were out, and they weren't moving. "Probably eating their government-issued dozen doughnuts in there," he said. "Fucken separatists." Wanda hefted herself over an icy part of the bank with her bare fingers. She said, "I don't even care anymore."

Henry liked finding himself in strangers' apartments. Wanda had almost no furniture. Just a mattress covered with a white duvet and three bookcases full of *Vogues*. She put her keys on one of the shelves and stepped out of her dress without any preamble. The dress stood like a tent, fading in and out of blue. The house, of course, was not heated, and when she spoke her breath streamed from her mouth like a cartoon bubble. She said, "I'm just going to set it to ambient."

Wanda flicked a couple of switches by the zipper at the back of her dress. She'd shaved all her hair, he noticed. Sometimes they did that, but not everything everything, like the head and everything. Especially eyebrows. That was really hardcore. He feigned indifference best he could. Hairless, yeah, that's cool. He practiced a few times in his head, Yeah, that's cool. That's cool.

The dress emitted a low, static hush, and projected a moon, complete with slanted, pockmarked face, on the wall opposite. "I can't sleep without white noise," she said.

"Yeah," said Henry, "that's cool." His breath funnelled toward the windows. At least a metre of breath ribboned out with every sentence, he estimated. He felt stupid standing there in his clothes, so he unbuckled his pants and unbuttoned his shirt and dropped them on the floor on top of his socks. Never mind the temperature, no one wants to see a naked man in socks. But he kept his snowflake shorts on, the finale, the final touch, and stood there, waiting, feeling bulky and hirsute. She reminded him of a beluga. He'd seen some belugas off the coast of Labrador a couple times. They were barely visible beneath the surface of the water. Then, like that, a flash of something translucent, with heft.

"You wear boxers," she said.

"Yeah," he answered. "Case I'm ever in a holdup and they make me strip. This way I'm covered." It was a line he threw around with girls when he dithered about taking off his underpants. This time the line seemed to throw itself. But the worry behind the phrase remained despite its overuse, the fear that he might be forced to expose himself in public.

Wanda moved closer to Henry. Warmth radiated from under their cold skin. It felt good. They kissed, and touched for a while. He told her she had the most amazing breasts. She said, "I know," and headed over to the bed, and he followed.

Wanda kept her eyes closed, which suited Henry. He'd already started thinking of her as alien girl. He was scoring with alien girl.

♈

Henry woke as Wanda brought him coffee she'd heated on a propane stove on the kitchen counter. He said thank you and sat up, not sure how to stick his finger through the little handle of the cup. He'd have to get out of there pretty fast. His colleagues were at the hotel. He didn't want them to find out.

If this was his apartment he'd cover up the windows, he thought, and told her, "If you covered up the windows it would be warmer in here."

"I know," she answered, "but I don't like to."

He nodded to the collection of magazines. "You have a lot of magazines." His mouth tasted disgusting. He wished he had some gum. He noticed the dress was turned off, or at least it wasn't humming or throwing moons anywhere anymore.

"I'm in a lot of them," she said. Her breath smoked around her face and dissipated in the intervals between her words. "I used to be a model. But I got tired of people looking at me. It's why I shave my hair off." Henry thought her ritual hair removal seemed only to exacerbate her little-girlhood vanity. And then he wondered if that's what he meant. Her words took up space in his head, like a glass full of ice cubes—That's why I shave my hair, that's why I shave, looking at me—then melted.

Wanda picked up a couple of the magazines and brought them to him, sitting beside him on the bed, tear-shaped breasts jiggling with every motion of her body. She seemed used to the cold and did not immediately join him under the covers. Instead she fanned pages over Henry's legs, and he saw pictures of her with sculpted hair, dressed in bodysuits, painted all over, kissing androgynous men, or hounds, or fat babies in Victorian carriages. Wanda said, "Look, the dress I had on last night, I copied it from this one. It's called The Eclipse. It's Valentino. It's the last job I had before I quit."

◈

They fucked again in the daylight. She was there and the bed was a warm nest he was loath to leave. January's noontime beams rubbed against the white walls, against the white sheets, against her clammy porcelain torso. Wanda's closed eyes blanked out her features so that only her tongue, like a slice of navel, protruded as demarcation. They bulked together, shivering, on the bed. A blush rose from between Wanda's breasts, up her neck and along her cheeks.

ICE STORM

The power knocked out midway through my stupid all-day, all-night Thursday shift and it got really cold inside my little *boutiquette*. Something popped behind the wall of *L'Homme rapaillé* inside of Ogilvy's department store and then came this profound stink—like Old Faithful was belching out skunks who died from eating rotten eggs—which ruined everything. A trickle of brown water started to snake along the tiles and we started hauling suits and talking fast, trying to hustle the old men out of there in a hurry. *Monsieur, Monsieur, Monsieur, s'il vous plaît!* That's my drama voice, part of an emphatic effort to head towards post-monochromatic speech. The sales associates, Marie-Audrey and Marie-Christine, had to broken-wrist-model-walk the men downstairs like border collies herding sheep. Good collies. You know, smart, groomed. Nice dogs. I'm not trying to say they're bitches.

I called the security booth. Hello, Number 14, please pick up. Mario, the old security booth guy, thought I was just a whiny shop kid but then a couple things happened. First: the jazz music they piped in went silent. Second: the lights. Then Mario believed me. And then Mario had to go and then I hung up.

Inside a blacked-out Ogilvy's, the racks of clothes and carpeting dark and silent as a forest underneath a bed of snow. When I was eleven, I was hanging behind a pharmacy in Westmount. I wasn't doing anything wrong. I thought of myself as a spiritual kind of kid, and I just liked watching the snow, you know. And when it started to snow I told myself: Remember Being Here. I would recite that phrase to myself like it was my own O Captain! My Captain! And time slowed to the pace of snowflakes moulting from the white sky, feathering into the parking lot, silencing even Sherbrooke Street. This is my snow reference point.

An alarm started to bleat from somewhere by the elevators down the hall. I got my stuff to go and clanged down the escalators. On the ground floor parquet, bouquet ladies in perfume shrieked a little bit and then shrieked some more when they heard themselves panic. While the clack-a-clack of their slingback kitten heels made haste, I was all hunching my shoulders in boredom in the half-light of the emergency lights, waiting around in line to go out the employee side door, and I saw this forty-something party girl from the Guerlain counter pocket a bottle of Shalimar on her way out. They never checked our pockets, just our bags. I had a tie down my pants so I wasn't gonna bust anyone on anything.

I got my routine purse investigation and lazy pat-down and walked past the department store's famous mechanical Christmas display, which was frozen in mid-action. Little bunnies teetering buckets over lodges, froggies gone a-fishin', monkeys working a flour mill—all at a standstill. The sky was bleak and its bleakness leaked into streets overrun with grey slush. Chunks of ice floated on roads shifted into sudden, sewer-spitting estuaries. Tanks had somehow appeared on the street corner since the time I'd started my shift. Whoa. Holy army going on.

People poured out of their extinguished buildings. The metro was shut down. A mass four o'clock exodus on foot. You never saw so many people in Montreal—it looked like a Philip Glass-orchestrated cityscape of New York. But maybe not even. Overweight buses stirred heavily past each stop, gainless and bulky as overdue pregnancies. All over downtown, lines lengthened, grew, strung out and around the sidewalks. The bus queues looked like an advertisement for affordable winter wear. They needed a soundtrack. They needed to spruce up. They needed new coats.

Ha. Sometimes I act all judgemental like that, like I don't need new duds all the time. It's bull. I just think I'm funny, even when I'm not. Someone's mom told me that once.

Funny or not, I was too poor to cab it, so it took me an hour and a half, walking cautiously over the icy sidewalks, to get from downtown to the cluster of low-rent buildings near the milk factory where I lived.

Whenever anyone asked where I lived, I told them it was right by the giant cow head and they knew what I meant and they had a story about how they used to give out ice cream there before. No one actually remembers eating it—it's always someone's friend's roommate's best friend's mother. Like that story about the dead dog in the suitcase.

DEAD DOG IN A SUITCASE

After doing her flight attendant safety routine in French, Joy told me about her last roommate who was taking care of a dog. The roommate shows up to walk the dog one morning and it's dead. So she calls the owners and they're all like, *Oh, we're sorry, it's not your fault, but could you please bring the dog to the vet and have it cremated.* So the roommate says okay. It's a little dog. It's the least she can do. She feels sort of bad even though it wasn't like she killed it. She looks around the house and finds a little suitcase to zip the dog into and she gets on the metro to go to the vet. On the metro, this guy starts talking to her, telling her she's cute and asking what's in the suitcase. Roommate says her computer and stuff, because he's weird and a dead dog in a suitcase is weird too. Next stop dude makes off with the dead dog suitcase.

I believed that dead dog story the first time I heard it. It reminded me a bit of that story about the burglars with the toothbrushes up their asses that I heard at Jesus Camp on Lake Massawippi. Sometimes it's nice to just believe something that sounds implausible, so you can freak out appropriately. Anyway, the ice cream story's like that. Like a pre-pasteurized milk when this was just a dairy kind of tale. Glory lore, like how everybody says they were at Woodstock. But that's okay. We all sort of remember lining up to get our cones. I remember it too, sometimes.

When I was a kid, my dad and I would drive out to the Italian neighbourhoods to see how they cabled their houses in the most brilliant displays of lights. But the ice covered Montreal—even in the neighbourhoods outside the core, so said the news, later, when I heard the news. So their lights were out too, probably. Into that dark night, mighty inflatable Santa Clauses, reindeer, and wires wrapped around curling banisters, blinking in on-off, on-off, on-off sections: stairs-window-balcony-balcony-stairs-stairs-window-balcony-balcony-stairs. They stopped doing that.

Instead, electrical wires draped low all along the streets, frosted and weighed down. I saw one cut and sparking on someone's lawn under a broken maple trunk. I could have gotten electrocuted but I didn't. It wasn't my time. Off-off, off-off, off-off.

On my block, a couple of sex workers paced in shiny gowns and running shoes. They must have been freezing. They were like high schoolers, you know, the defiance of their undress boldly stating: I don't need a hat! I don't need winter boots! I don't feel the cold like you do! And they were preening in their scrappy outfits like they were anywhere else but on the border of NDG and the City of Montreal West in the Time of the Great and Cold Fiasco. One woman chugged back a two-litre carton of chocolate milk. A Montreal West dude in a muscle car, a real hero sandwich, skidded by shouting that she should "get a real job!" The woman took another swig from the carton, hitched up her skirt over her tube socks, and said, "I'm doing the best I know how," and horked out some milk and phlegm into the street.

Watching her, I thought, I never learned how to properly hork. No Leonardo ever taught me how to spit. You know what happens when you think about a James Cameron movie? The universe will punish you. One exception. No. Two exceptions: you're allowed to say, or think, "I'll be back," and also, "Hasta la vista, baby," because they're ironic sentences to throw around, because Arnold Schwarzenegger is too weird to deprive yourself of making fun of him. Because you WANT to sound like a moron when you say that. Anything else, there's payback. Proof: I thought, and kind of enviously, too, of Leonardo DiCaprio teaching Kate Winslet how to spit off the fancy deck of the Titanic, and I immediately fell on my ass and thwacked my head on the sidewalk. A skating rink-style sidewalk, you know, a total sheet of ice. No blood. But a nice fat wet stain spread on the seat of my pants like I'd pissed myself. It was lame that I'd managed to get all the way to my front stoop without falling before I did.

It's sort of like how the old people at my church talk about this fighter pilot from WWII who made it through the war, through a POW camp in Germany, only to die in a wreck when the old Grand Boulevard streetcar hit his cab on the way home from the airport after V Day. There's some element of destiny there.

At home I flicked the hall light switch. It didn't work. I tried the other. It didn't work.

"Hey, lady."

Jordan sat on the futon, naked except for his checked robe and his Bart Simpson slippers. I didn't like the slippers. Slippers shouldn't have faces. Jordan lit a candle with his lighter flame on high, and then his cigarette from the wick.

"Looks like you had a little accident, Marlene. Playing hide and seek again?"

"Fell." I used to get nervous and pee myself when I played hide and go seek. It happens to people sometimes.

"We've got an island-wide power outage going on. You want some drinks?"

I ignored him. Because he was naked and also because of the peeing my pants thing.

I'm not trying to set you up to dislike him. When he wasn't all dishclothy or high he could be pretty smart. He went to Brown. He has pretty eyelashes. And the way he has about knowing he's gonna get his way with things is sort of addictive to watch. It's a talent. It goes beyond intuition. Like a gifted sense of arrogance that always pans out.

Jordan used to steal my Barbies and hack at them with his stepfather's silver-handled steak knife collection. He'd tell me it was the Viet Congs that'd tortured them. I let him do it, sometimes, because after, we'd lip-synch to Debbie Gibson together beside his mother's grand piano. I'd never have had the balls to rip up my dolls without him.

I went to my room and lay on my unmade bed in my wet clothes. Seagulls fought by a garbage can outside my window. I felt inundated with things to do and the sensation of time running out on me, weeks and weekends and work weeks. I couldn't keep track. Months adding up, hair growing, nail biting, shaving, throwing out old things that used to be new. Buying soap. Fucking Dove soap. Time and time and time and time and time and time and time and time and time. I needed an Air Supply version of that to cheer me up.

I didn't expect things to go so belly-up in my middle age. But I'm a Scorpio and, according to a friend who did my chart—well she's maybe not my friend, she's a Swedish girl from work who kind of looks like me—I just allow things to happen. I'm not ambitious enough, which is probably true. A psychic once told me I should learn how to make lists and also to wear copper in my shoes to ground my energy. He said I should use pennies. But pennies in my shoes reminded me of that goody-goody from elementary school who wore penny loafers for picture day every year. I should have been Dorothy in *The Wizard of Oz* instead of that goody-good. Just saying. I wish my music teacher could have considered that there might be a reason I was handing my Sibelius project in late—like maybe my mom had gone on one of her long sherry samplings and I wasn't just being some preteen twat. She shouldn't have punished me by giving the part of Dorothy to that goody-good. I don't think it's crazy to say that my life would have been pretty different if I'd been Dorothy. Instead I played the synthesizer.

There was a certain stagehand appeal to the synthesizer, of course. Plus I had little boob nubs that year. I wore suspenders over them. I carted the synthesizer on the bus and felt pretty cool, with my nubs and my suspenders and my case. I felt like hot shit at the exact same time that I was more mad than jealous about the Dorothy part being pretty much stolen from me. It still made me mad and I hated that goody-good as I kept on thinking about coffee.

I wasn't planning on making actual coffee. I was planning on drinking instant coffee. To be even more precise: instant decaf. Which might seem like a replica of a replica but that's not thinking. This is how it is. You have to understand there are simply different categories of hot drinks. You don't judge them. You say to yourself, sure, espresso is best. You drink espresso to feel that there is a reason to be wherever you are. Say, at Olive and Gourmando in Old Montreal, sometime between ten and eleven-thirty on a weekday, and you deserve to look at the art student waitresses with their asymmetrical haircuts and see-through pants. This espresso tableau exists for you. But also, this is fatuous living, this is living fatuously, and maybe it's just not for every day. Who can be a pasha every day?

FILTER COFFEE: The coffee of the people. Usually under two bucks, the way things should be. Also, many places (though not the Oxford Café) will give you free refills.

CHURCH COFFEE: Almost as good as hot chocolate. Not

taste-wise, memory-wise. Remember drinking this coffee. You know everyone loves you, you are at the Sunday school, there are cookies. Creator God. John Wesley. Hymns. The Blue Room. It's good. It's great.

INSTANT COFFEE: And its fraternal twin, instant decaf. Instant coffee is a good bachelor drink. You could be a hobo, waiting for a boxcar, drinking your instant coffee in a tin cup, playing with the mouth organ and leftover tobacco in your pocket with your free hand. You are sort of like in *The Grapes of Wrath*, if the Joads could have had instant coffee instead of that spurting breast milk business. They'd have dug it. You are digging it for them. And that's a class all its own.

TEA: I never mentioned tea. Should tea go between espresso and instant decaf? Or have its own category? This should be a diagram and not a paragraph. Because, also, there are so many teas. As many teas as there are leaves and flowers. But we can forget about the tisanes and the egg net things and talk real tea bags you buy in cardboard boxes. You begin with Salada, which is like church coffee, a great comfort. There's also Red Rose, Salada's kissing cousin, which provides almost the same stalwart support as Salada except the picture on the box is prettier, because it's a flower, plus it's a good story, the one it reminds us of, the story of Rose Red. And then there's Lady Grey. That's rich lady morning tea. And Irish Breakfast is more Sunday morning.

There was a bang at the door. There were a few. I didn't

want to face that old mophandler Angel about the rent. Not then. We still had till the twenty-second before we had to pay. But Jordan couldn't be diplomatic. In November he'd yelled through the door that he wished he could just be a prince. Angel's English wasn't good enough to understand that meant Jordan wasn't paying up. Then the landlord tacked something about an eviction on the door. I was embarrassed. Meh, I was all-out shamed. The neighbours saw. Even the weird guy without the eyebrows upstairs saw. Finally, Jordan's dad, and his dad lives in Latvia or Mesopotamia or something, came through for us. "I told him he owes me from the divorce, still," Jordan said. I said, "Dude, your parents got divorced when you were eight." He said, "Yeah, and my dad hardly gave me any money for college and so he owes me. Plus I'm his kid. Plus I like living like I'm on heroin."

Bo looked back at me all fish-eyed and backlit through the peephole. "I forgot you were coming over," I said, happy to see her face stretching out towards my eye in bubblicious Christmas ornament exaggeration.

"I tried to call to remind you but your phone isn't working. Open up!"

I did. And hung in the doorframe. Lanky-like. "It was disconnected a while ago."

"You should get a cellphone, already. You don't have power? Neither do my parents. Let me in. I have bagels." She said bagels with a private school girl accent, like she was too bored to say bagels. She pushed open the door and tried to duck under my arm.

"Okay, yeah. Hey. It's good to see you. Come in my room, I'm making coffee."

She took off her boots. She shouldn't have bothered. The floor was filthy. Course it was also pretty dark, so she probably couldn't tell. I was in the process of trying to train Jordan out of letting me do all the cleaning. It wasn't going so well.

"Is that a camping stove? In your room? Careful you don't blow your whole apartment. Shit, Marlene. You can't live here like this. Is your toilet at least still flushing?"

"Last I dumped."

"Gross. Also, like totally unnecessary info. You guys live like squatters."

"I wish!" Jordan called out from the living room.

"What is he even doing in there?"

"Thinking about Bauhaus!" he yelled.

So we sat on my mattress. Bo kept her grandmother's old fur coat on. Ding dong, she looked like a furbell, a tinker, a tinker bell, a ding dong the witch is dead belle. "Look! I can see my breath! That's crazy." She pulled a beret out of her pocket and stuck it over the intricate buns pinned to her head. The water boiled. I poured it over some spacey dehydrated granules, added Jack Daniels and a dash of coffee whitener. Because a dash makes it dashing. A splash makes it splashing. She was still so girlish. Round cheeks, pudgy belly stretched over her wide hips, elegant toes. Fertility goddess circa 1942. I handed her a cup. She gagged.

"You're just a coffee snob from those swanky Laurier pâtisseries you work at."

"I know I am, but what are you?" She eyed me, raising her eyebrows. She plucked her eyebrows superfine. I wouldn't have liked it on anyone else but her. On her it was little girl cute, classic milkmaid Coca-Cola ad.

"I practically had to skate my way here," she said.

"Is that why you have so many clothes on? What do you have underneath all these layers?"

"And you never even call me."

I grabbed at her hat. I could imagine Bo's usual array of second-hand undergarments smelling somewhat enticingly of someone else's musk. Plus she wasn't all that keen on the washing up. Her and her friends thought their hair and their ears just washed themselves, or they made their own shampoo out of baking soda. I always said what you're supposed to say about body hair and maintenance, though. *T'es belle. T'es belle comme tu es.* And she was, and a lot of it was that *au naturel* glow she had. But she could stand to shave her legs sometimes. I'm just saying. It could be I'm being pissy in retrospect, but let us allow for the opposite, that maybe distance can give me some clearer judgement than I had at the time.

Bo put her cup on the floor and unbuttoned her fur coat. She put on a French-from-France accent. *Très sexy.* "To begin with, we have zis little dress vith polka dots." Bo's breath was several coffees sour and her little kisses were sloppy, delivered with open-mouthed vehemence and urgent noises, like she was acting out passion. I let myself be an object for her arousal until she had my shirt off. We goosebumped. She has great breasts. Dense and round.

Once I told her I thought she had denser boobs because of all the coffee she drank but she never believed me. She turned around. Her ass wavered in a pair of old-fashioned bloomers, her skin milky, glowing against the bare mattress in the dark room. I bit. She hollered, but I think it was because she liked it.

In the morning sleet blurred the windows. Bo slept mummified in my sleeping bag, turned away from me. I got up, lit a match and started the stove up. Bo grunted a mouthful of muffled consonants—*grhfrrcdr*-something and rolled—that kind of snappy body language I know I'm in trouble when I see.

"What."

"I'm not having any more of your instant things," Bo said, still under the sleeping bag. "Real food or nothing."

"There are your bagels. And some chocolate puddings. Shit. I forgot the fridge isn't working. I also have sauerkraut. Would you like some sauerkraut for breakfast?" Bo murmel murmel murmelled. I went to the kitchen and came back with a couple of puddings and plastic measuring spoons. Bo emerged from the sleeping bag like a turtle extending its neck. Or like the way ET stretches his neck. Except way prettier. Way, way more.

"It's clammy in here," she said.

"Can I borrow your phone? I should see if the store is open today."

Bo handed it over.

There was an automated message that we'd be shut down for a while, which was good because I felt discouraged just thinking about another walk into the city. "Work's closed. Maybe I should quit, anyway."

She sat up. Her eyes skipped over me. "Why don't you go back to university so you can do something you like better?"

"I'm too old." My usual rebuttal: Poor me. Cue *Love Story* theme. Do that thing with your arms where you're playing the violin at me.

"Do music." See? She read my mind.

"Nah, not good enough anymore. You have to be pretty perfect, you know, it's not like it's something you do cuz it's making you feel good, like baking a plate of cookies, or knitting a half-assed scarf to feel crafty."

"I think you're tired of selling suits at Ogilvy's. You've been doing it for a decade. Why don't you just do something else?" Bo was pulling on her fishnets. She lit a Peter Jackson. "Don't you think that, like, you draw these circumstances to yourself?"

"What—like the goddamn ice storm? What do you mean?"

"Marlene, I have a biology exam today . . . if school hasn't been cancelled."

I thought of that line from that hymn—What shall I bring him, poor as I am? If I were a shepherd, I would bring a lamp. A lamb. I continued eating my chocolate pudding with my tablespoon. If I were a pudding-eater I would bring pudding and a spoon.

"Here, have mine too," she said, handing me back the cup.

THE DIFFERENT FLAVOURS OF PRIM

The Eastern European kind, with complicated French braids twisted neatly around their heads, old-world country girl style, who dress in buttoned-up shirts and high-waisted skirts that have no purposeful link to retro. Their faces are plain as Mormons or Mennonites and you can tell they know how to scrub a thing clean. I worked at the same store with a girl like that, once, who told me her mother put blue powder on her arm when she broke it. What does that even mean, blue powder on broken bones?

Beyond stoicism.

There are the hard-studying Protestant girls—they're the mainstay of classical music. They consider their appearance, they're upper-middle class taken down a notch.

It's their movements that belie their prudery. Gestures sharp as protractored designs. A value of thoughtfulness, a Christian-tinged, politically correct way of speaking that at its heart I'm cool with but it's somehow thickened in the distance between authenticity and socialization that these girls are lost to themselves. I hate how they're cotton-battened stiff-upper-lipped and they feel if they can just memorize the rules they'll have an underhanded upper hand, an outward appearance of evenhandedness, they'll be well turned out. I was one of those. I feigned innocence all the time and got away with it. I prompted myself into sincerity to match my appearance. I look pretty innocuous. You'd say so too. If you met me.

PRODS

The Prods make me sad, that I've said too much, the world seems loose, sort of depressed sad, like there is no grand master plan, just a lot of busy bees kind of sad, whereas the Eastern European kind point me to a life full of invigorating tragedy I've never known—emigrating-on-cargo-ships-style calamity. The Protestant girls are as much about stuff as the Eastern European ones are about leaving everything behind. When I say Prod, sometimes I mean Anglo, but sometimes I change my mind about that.

Bo wore frocks. I don't even know where she got all the costumey stuff she decked herself out with. She smoked too much and she was always recovering from a case of bronchitis. She was second-generation Hungarian hot, of the ugly-is-the-new-beautiful variety. It hurt my teeth to look at her straight on. Remember

Being Here. Sometimes I grind my teeth at night, when I'm having sexy dreams. That's probably where I got the teeth thing.

Anyway. It was lame. Because I used to know how to woo. Maybe. Hey, you can't exactly prove me wrong on that.

I HAVE SHORT HAIR

I call a meeting. Chelsea looks at her phone the whole time. Her Facebook's full of pretty countryside girls. Where she's from she's a pretty girl. I picture her in high school. I don't know what I imagine. Simple, straightforward, nice people in the country? Maybe she was popular and bitchy? I can't tell.

Chelsea glances up after I finish talking about the schedule. "Oh my god," she says. "I'm just looking at your jacket. It's so funny. You must be the only person who can wear that kind of thing."

The light streams in through the glass walls of the meeting room from across the hall. It's blinding.

A man in crutches lurches up to the open door and asks us where SEO sits.

❧

Someone finally got a kettle. We get free tea. It's a good deal. I can drink a lot of free tea. Especially ever since I got colitis and can't drink coffee anymore.

I woke up late. I almost always wake up late. And then Ben likes it when I spoon him. So I do, and we wind up too hot in the blankets and groping and I jump out of bed looking messed up with no time to spare for styling my hair or wiping off the remains of last night's mascara. I leave Ben with his cereal, oats, nuts, fruit, coffee, and laptop as I leave, resenting him his day a little, enjoying being outside, regretting having to get up, lying to myself that I can make the 9:42 metro when it's 9:37 and it takes me twelve minutes to walk to the station from our apartment. I could walk faster, but I get bogged down looking around. The elderly woman who walks her German Shepherd every morning by the new bar on Notre Dame. The bearded dad with his two kids in a stroller. If they're already over the tracks when I see them I'm definitely late. I check out who's at the cafés, how many cabs are at the stand, how the park is looking, what's going on in the winter sky.

I get to work and I'm at the tea stand in the hall. Moroccan oil girl comes up to me. "I finally got my glamour pics done," she tells me, her tone kind of hushed.

The water has almost boiled. I rip the tag off the tea bag, and cut off most of the string, too, so it doesn't look like a tampon—the mouse's tail, Ben calls it.

"Glamour pics? Like modelling?"

"But without clothes on. I found the guy on Craigslist. I told myself for years I'd do this, and I just decided now was the time."

"No time like the present."

Dunk, dunk, dunk the little tea bags in and out of the paper cups.

"He told me to do my own hair and makeup. It took like two hours."

"Cool." Sprinkle in the Splenda. Tap, tap, tap.

"A friend came with me, you know, Roxanne, from work."

"Safer that way, I guess. I'm sure she's great with makeup."

Moroccan oil girl says, "Your boyfriend doesn't mind you have short hair?"

"He gets pretty confused. Sometimes he thinks I'm a man," I tell her. Stir, stir, stir.

There's no mistaking me for a man—not that I don't covet those lanky Charlotte Gainsbourg androgynous features. I do. My melancholy would suit that bony body, the stubborn set of jaw. But I have the figure of a WASPy mid-century housewife.

"I can see how that could happen," she says, sympathetic. So nice.

Wrath seizes me up quick. I swallow every sarcastic remark. Force a giant grin. I tell myself I look like the girl who's supposed to be smiling and inclusive and happy. Cheerleader-style. They get mad if I don't give it to them. Grin a big fucking grin. It's so nice being told I don't look feminine! Love it! I'd never tell her her highlights look cheap and every plastic thing she's wearing looks like shit. I'm a four-year-old whining *it's not fair it's not fair it's not fair*. Sip, sip, sip.

Back to the mag, my two screens, light filtering off the highway into our office. It's eye-hurtingly brilliant, glorious, the highways far below our office, serpenting chrome and asphalt and fast food chains. You can't hear them. You can just hear the computer programmers cawing to each other like a murder of crows, something they do, and the ventilation shafts whirring, and the social media team in the next room erupting into giggles. One of them says she kissed Corey Haim, once. She asks her summer intern, "Did you ever kiss someone who died?"

❧

We're always in the bathroom at the same time.

"I could never have short hair like that! I would just worry about not looking pretty, I guess. When are you growing it out?"

I have baby hair. Don't have the option for long, lustrous locks. There's no growing this out.

Her eyes, a genuine goodness I've rarely encountered. It's moving, but also it requires that you constantly move towards her emotionally, to explain all the things she doesn't understand. There is rarely repartee.

"I'm not growing it out."

"Oh, that's different."

"My mom has short hair. She had three husbands." Probably I shouldn't have said that. Roxanne doesn't know what to say. I'm an asshole. I'm a total jerkface.

On Facebook her name is Roxy Almost Famous Monaghan.

❧

Monday morning meeting. My boss says, "I hate women who have short hair." He says this looking directly at the only out woman on our floor, whose hair is swept up in a glossy platinum pompadour.

"Come on," I say.

"I knew you were going to say something," he says, turning towards me and smiling. He thinks he's being charming.

"You're the one exception. You can carry off short hair because you're pretty. I hate it on everyone else."

It's so problematic, him calling me pretty in front of the other girl, like she's not. Him telling me I'm pretty at all. Him saying that at work, in front of colleagues.

Everyone likes her more than me, she's more likeable, but outgoing in a way that exhausts me. He hates her. I think it's because she's gay, because she's not playing the long-haired princess role.

"Thanks for telling me I'm pretty, Frank," I say, trying to make a joke of it. My voice is flat. I grin the big fucking motherfucker grin.

❧

"Can you make sure the post about hottest celebrity cleavages goes up today?" I ICQ Tara in social media. Tara is as birdlike as an Olsen twin. Her features are lost under her sculpted makeup.

"KKK!" she answers.

"Thanks! ☺ ☺"

"NPOI!"

"I mean NP!! ☺ ☺ ☺ ☺" she says.

"☺ ☺" I say.

"☺ ☺ ☺ ☺" she says.

❧

"You fucking cunt!" I yell at a woman who almost mows me down. She turned left on a red and tried to squeal her way onto the highway. She didn't see me. I have never called anyone a fucking cunt before.

She comes to a stop. We make eye contact. Her face is livid.

I cross the road and go to the Indian diner.

"Lentil non-fried bread?" the guy asks.

"Lentil non-fried bread," I say.

❧

"You're wearing a hat to work?"

"My hair looked so bad this morning! I had to cover it!"

"So that's why you're wearing a hat? It's not that cold?"

"Yup!"

"Sleaze leads," someone behind us says to someone else.

❧

"If we were the cast of *Community*, Jessica would be Annie Edison."

"Totally!"

"You know what she said to me? She said her friends do crazy things, too."

"Like what? Play Scrabble? Sing in the choir?"

I wish I was in a choir. I suck at Scrabble.

The two rich country girls living it up on the Plateau are talking about me where I can hear them.

I hate looking like such a fucking WASP.

There are worse problems. It sucks looking rich, I wish I looked put-together and rich.

❧

My friend Bethany is a nun. She's younger than me. A large silver cross dangles over her T-shirt. It's inscribed with two words: "pax" across, and "caritas" down. Latin for "peace" and "love." She's only in town for the morning. We meet at the Tim Hortons before I head to the office. She orders a coffee. A double-double.

Which is so normal, considering she's a nun.

I feel myself slumping. Writer troll posture, we call it at work. My skin is grimy from the highways. She is humble, radiant.

ঞ৹৹

She's a few stairs in front of me. I notice her strappy green sandals, her yellow circle purse. I look up. I realize I know her. We used to be roommates.

Seeing a friend completely undoes me. I start to cry. At the top of the escalator, I say, "I hate my job."

Justine and I walk across the highway to grab a coffee at Tim Hortons. She's startled but sympathetic. She has to get to the auction house before ten.

ঞ৹৹

I walk into the conference room. Gossip hangs around like a stink. A flare.

BREW

Clotilde soaked slices of spongy white dépanneur bread in bowls of warm milk in the mornings. It smelled like baby food. At dinnertime her arm levered out soup or $1.99-a-can mushroom and garlic spaghetti sauce onto my plate, her square hand handing me cutlery, napkins, cheese.

When Clotilde was sick she concocted brews of mint tea and tiger balm, drinking them out of second-hand ceramic Japanese bowls set aside especially for this purpose. She lay in her room for days, skipping her journalism classes, stinking up the house with dollar-store incense.

She hennaed her hair each month with a shade called Sunset Red. She handed in her essays on parchment dyed in black tea and was astounded that she almost failed her political science class when she'd gone to the trouble of scribing her term paper with a quill.

During the ice storm, Clotilde invited an entire contingent of foreign exchange students to stay at our apartment. We lived in front of a defunct old-age home—our wires were buried deep beneath the ground—and we still had electricity.

The entire city was closed. Our classes were cancelled, the coffee shop I worked at was closed, and we spent almost every moment of that week together.

I was the first to wake each morning. Momentarily alone, I swept the floors and prepped café au laits for everyone.

On the Wednesday of that week, Clotilde complained, groggily, "You woke us up. You were laughing in your sleep."

The Italian countess, Giulia, a real countess, who shared Clotilde's single bed—they slept head-to-toe, for the duration of the storm—got up long after the Brazilian theatre students, to whom I was invisible. I wore plaid shirts and too much Mountain Equipment Co-op as a result of my years out west.

I made more espresso and warmed more milk, as though in absence of my barista job I could find nothing better to do.

The countess had thick black hair. Her haphazardly worn Yves Saint Laurent and the diamond ring that looped around her finger were props from a life I knew nothing of. She had olive skin and constellations of moles along her neck and chest that peeked out with the movements of her cotton kimono. She was four and a half months pregnant, her stomach smooth and hard as a waterworked stone. Her pregnancy tired her, as did the circumstances—the cold, the army, the ice. She passed the time telling us stories about how she'd met her fiancé, a philanthropist poet who was waiting for her at his family estate in Torino. They'd met at a wedding in Dublin.

She rubbed cocoa butter over her stomach each morning to prevent stretch marks and misted her wrists with amber perfume. "It is essential to discover your signature scent," she told me.

The week wore itself out, the power came back, and eventually everyone dispersed.

I never saw any of them again.

I never found a perfume I liked.

STATIONS OF THE CROSS

She'd lived here, once. Some time ago. Between the ages of nineteen and twenty-seven. Eight years. (She had to count on her hands to be sure.)

Emmanuelle liked to say she'd worked every job. Of course that wasn't true, but she had bounced between a number of *jobbines* throughout her over-extended BA and MA stretch. She'd worked in bars and flower shops and big chain grocery stores. She'd slopped greasy lasagna into Styrofoam platters in underground metro malls, she'd grilled chicken and pesto paninis, scrubbed dishes, taught accountants English as a second language, graded exams, Xeroxed course packs, read palms on the side.

After completing her Master's in Communications, she landed her first full-time professional gig at an ad agency in Mississauga. She piled all her half-broken furniture out on the curb in front of her building with a sign that said "GRATUIT – FREE," moved her couple of suitcases of possessions and started what she considered her proper grown-up life in earnest there.

It was far enough from Montreal. It was even farther from the Eastern Township town where she'd been brought up. It wasn't Toronto but it was close. She rose through the ranks at her job at the agency, content, after her multitude of part-time half-jobs, to sink her teeth into something that felt like what she ought to be doing. She'd grown tired of being jostled. She was, in fact, very tired from her student years' hustles.

After a while, Emmanuelle was able to put a down payment down on a one-bedroom rent-to-own condo.

She wore work-appropriate fit-and-flare dresses with matching kitten heels.

She led a team of fifteen content creators efficiently enough.

She came home to her glass of Italian red after a long day and caught up on her TV.

The years slipped by.

Emmanuelle hadn't returned to Montreal in twelve years, not since her grad school commencement. But now her job was sending her on a four-day creative summit titled "Content Creation and the Future of Marketing."

Emmanuelle had been reminiscing and anticipating the trip for weeks, but almost as soon as she stepped off the train she found it excruciating to be back.

Walking through the city where she'd lived in her twenties was like pacing through an exercise of penance. Certain locations were physically exacting to see again; a reaction she had not calculated in the countdown of her anticipation.

While not setting out to trace sites of her life's humiliations, Emmanuelle would happen upon them as she made her way from a coffee shop to a grocery store, from the McGill metro station back to her room at the Delta.

The city was full of reminders of an endless strain of indiscretions related mostly to soured romances. Which was itself another foolishness. An uncontained libido, a hungry body, an exciting and far-less-than-exciting series of non-love stories that left all parties dumped and there was possibly puke or tears involved because sex can bring on strong emotions, like too much liquor. Even if at first you think it's fine, it's no big deal, I can handle it. A couple shots in and you're out.

In front of this downtown pseudo-Irish sports bar Emmanuelle had fought, drunk—she must have been drunk since she couldn't remember a single thing she'd been arguing about. She'd been fighting with a boyfriend she was trying to break up with while simultaneously fighting with herself as she tried not to want to take him home with her. They quarrelled outside for too long. They argued, loudly, drunkenly, stupidly in front of crowds, shoving tourists and packs of half-naked, singing froshers. She had no recollection of any words she and her thenboyfriend had exchanged in their clash, she could only recall how she'd felt. And she felt it, palpably, immediately, right now. It felt as if beneath whatever words they spoke he was saying, *We need to go home together* and she knew they should and she resisted it and it didn't make sense to either of them that she was arguing with him about something that should have been simple. He called and wrote and emailed and sent her a card in the mail but the next time she saw him was at another bar, and she ducked out, heart beating hard. She was scared. Of him, of herself, of her shame. Now, years later, she thought about him with regret. Regret at her misplaced priorities, regret at hurting someone with whom she had shared such lovely times. They had walked in the countryside, cycled on an island in the river, eaten ice cream; he'd made her pumpkin pie from scratch for her birthday. Twice, in fact. Twice in one week he'd made the pie. She dashed it for a panicked series of ideas that had never panned out. She had told him, in an email, *There is no love here!*

And it was true. But it was still nice. And it was still too bad.

On the Monday of the conference, at her first dinner out with the other content managers, they'd been booked for a dinner at the same East End restaurant where Emmanuelle had been taken out after a vernissage, years ago, and the man she'd gone with then had flirted with the gallery assistant in front of her, going to the trouble of leaning over Emmanuelle to flirt with the gallery assistant, saying something to her about the band Roxette, which she was too young to know about anyway, and the assistant flushed while everyone else at the table witnessed the awkwardness of the situation, sipped their liquor quietly.

Another night, after the team-building fraternization exercise—an escape room; a few hours of feigned competition, feigned excitement, some sweatiness, boredom—her group of colleagues headed out to a comedy act in the theatre district.

Emmanuelle found herself beside the theatre where she had learned—how stupid she had been for her not knowing this at the time, at the advanced age of almost thirty—not to disclose someone's medical condition out loud. An entire friend group from her political science class had disowned her after she'd asked about someone's health when she shouldn't have, and whenever she thought of them, even now, a dozen years later, she felt a red-alert level of deep, abiding shame, and still she hated herself for not having known something as obvious as that, she felt provincial and stupid and ridiculous for treading so indelicately, for being such a bull in a china shop with private information, for lacking empathy and being unintentionally cruel; worse, a gossip. It was also the experience that had shown her something that would continue: women's rage against her, a kind of how-dare-you shaming that persisted still. Emmanuelle hadn't been able to concentrate on the comedy show. "I'm just tired," she told the group in the cab back to the hotel. But really she felt the shame of that long-ago event as palpably as if it had just occurred. Her heart beat in her ears.

One weekday morning she visited a friend from university who'd bought an upper duplex in Outremont and given birth to an adorable towheaded baby. Their reunion had verged on dull. The baby woke up and didn't like strangers, didn't like Emmanuelle's glasses, and Emmanuelle was asked to remove them, and then the baby had to be fed, burped, changed, and put down for a nap. After leaving her friend and her friend's blonde child, Emmanuelle walked past the industrial loft by the tracks where she'd once worn a short jean dress and pink and white underwear with little bows on the sides just in case she'd picked someone up at the concert they were attending. Who wore underpants with bows. Who bought second-hand underpants. She remembered giggling with a woman who later became a how-dare-you accuser. She remembered the soft slant of summer's evening sunlight hitting the bridges of their noses and warming their similarly freckled shoulder blades. She had lifted up her dress to show her friend the underpants, laughing.

On this grass in this nearby park she had lain down and kissed a far younger than her architecture student—he was barely old enough to drink. He was in an open relationship with another woman, a fibre arts student from his school. He said he liked her, the fibre arts student, because of her squirrel face. Emmanuelle and the architecture student had lain down and kissed in front of Hasidic women and their children, not minding if they saw. The Hasidic moms watched them unblinkingly. They didn't turn away. She remembered that.

In another park nearby she'd been hot for a taxi driver she'd met on an escalator—he was going up and she was going down, or maybe it was the other way around? They'd made eye contact, bumped into each other later, and begun to sleep together shortly afterwards. And maybe it was the same week as the architecture student, she couldn't remember anymore, but she'd made out with the taxi driver in front of kids playing, made out too much, too publicly.

Around the corner from that park is where she took someone for bagels in an attempt to find the Hasidic kissing park. She'd gotten lost and they had a bad time picnicking in someone's yard or a parking lot instead. The date had headed south early and she had very much wanted it to go another way.

This alleyway is where Emmanuelle had emerged from a love declaration from a partner only to bump into the only woman she'd ever taken home. The woman's adorable little peanut face perplexed at Emmanuelle's stammering reaction.

In front of this new condo development downtown, she and the taxi driver had stopped and straddled their similarly old fashioned bikes and he thought she wanted an open relationship and she thought he wanted an open relationship and she let him say that that was what he wanted and so she strayed and then ghosted him a year later.

They had also fought and she had yelled at him on a North-South street that cracked the city in half and it embarrassed her that they fought in public and she remembered that he told her that her essays were bad, he'd said she should try harder. One time when they'd been having sex he'd rubbed his car keys on her and that was horribly embarrassing to think about now.

The man who she dated who'd since been accused of multiple

acts of sexual aggression. It had been in the news, lately. She'd dated him even though he'd left her outside his apartment, right there, by the grocery store, waiting in the cold, night after night, as he steeled himself to invite her inside. That year, she'd thought people would fall in love with her and change their lives to be with her. She thought falling in love was the norm. She was surprised when she stopped moving people.

The time she had the miscarriage and she didn't know who the father would have been, the one whose family had been in the *schmatta* industry and owned the house near the Hasidic park or the taxi driver who spoke silly things to her in Russian to make her laugh. Though she'd never thought she had a type, the two men didn't look unlike each other. The baby, had there been one, could have looked like either man. She would have had to ask them to take a paternity test to know for certain. How embarrassing. She sobbed at the first's apartment. He said, *It would have been nice to have a baby with you.* She sobbed with the other when he brought her pho and he was the one who she really thought was responsible for the little shrimpish looking creation she'd expelled after a great deal of pain and dark purple blood and he said, *I would never have been part of that you'd definitely be on your own with this.* Which is possibly why she eventually ghosted him. It was either that or because of a drummer. She liked the idea of the tepid one better. He was more beautiful and educated and stylish but their intimacy was vague and somehow petty. It was tinged in regretful sadness and afterwards he often spoke about his academic ex and how they might get back together. And when Emmanuelle got dressed again (she never slept over) his roommate had leered at her contemptuously, pouring portions of dinner slop—they called it slop—

onto plates for himself and his friend, who would then, she assumed, discuss her. She was horribly dressed back then, often wearing a shapeless grey dress from a garage sale from behind the carpet store where she worked. She'd felt hopeless that she'd ever be able to afford nice clothes.

Around the corner from the hippy coffee shop that had worn a dozen names over the last twenty years but the same patchouli clientele, she went to a party where everyone's girlfriends moved protectively closer to their boyfriends when she spoke to them. One woman, a celebrated poet, spoke of her husband with reverence and everyone glowed as she did. That's when Emmanuelle realized she'd have to have this sort of pairing off to be considered safe and out of the way. Respectable.

Nearby, by the metro station, was the apartment where she had been carried into the bedroom night after night. Not far from the apartment where the roommate had leered while serving slop. Parallel to it, in fact, and around the corner from where she had lived in her early twenties, in a purple room decorated with Wiccan incantations. Another shame. More ridiculousness.

She'd walked here, up this street near the Hasidic neighbourhood, in a complete downpour and through inches of water that ran from gutters over her new shoes which she felt she should never have bought because she never wanted to wear leather again because she could picture the cow's eyes knowing it would be slaughtered and couldn't handle causing extinction for footwear.

This is where she went on a date with a man from the coffee shop she worked at when she was nineteen years old who touched her horribly cut short wannabe pixie looking like a buzz and her tough face and her no money in her waitress shoes and pyjama pants and he had said, *Your pants are kind of weird.* His private school togetherness, his Mediterranean handsomeness, so far beyond her.

Down the street from another park further east where a friend had slammed a door in her face one morning upon guessing where she'd spent the night.

She remembered the hunger she felt in those years. Like some baby vampire waking famished, gluttonous, choosing carelessly and exuberantly, sampling all kinds of people indiscriminately, never guessing there were consequences. She couldn't know. Because before that she had been asleep. Deeply asleep. To all things that moved or could move her or anyone.

Now she was awake and the scenes from her memories haunted her. They layered over what she viewed as she walked, doubling, filtering what she saw.

She headed over to the old-fashioned diner turned retro-on-purpose and ordered a matzo ball soup. It tasted the same as it had before the restaurant's renovations. Kids in their twenties garbed in oddly fitting second-hand clothes, adorable youth costumes, flirted voraciously around her, gregarious and beautiful. The sound of their energy humming, vibrant, alive.

PREVIOUSLY PUBLISHED:

Versions of some of these stories have been published in other publications.

"Rivière Rouge" and "Number 42" were published in *Pistol Press* Vol. 1, 2008.

"The Intrusion" and "The Shakes" were published in *Snafu Anthology* Issue 1, 2008.

"Brew," "Chez Serge," "Embouchure," "Spam," and "The End," appear in a chapbook titled *Eating Out* published by WithWords Press, 2010.

"Downpour" was published in *Swamp* magazine, 2011.

"The Knockoff Eclipse" appeared in *Branch* magazine, 2012.

"Parc Lafontaine" was published in *Maisonneuve* magazine, 2012.

"Directions" was published in *Matrix Magazine*, 2015.

"Ice Storm" was published in *Joyland*, 2017.

ACKNOWLEDGEMENTS:

For close reads, edits, or proofs of the individual stories or · manuscript at various stages, huge thanks to Andrea Bennett, Shanti Maharaj, Maxime Raymond Bock, Anna Leventhal, Sean Michaels, Jeff Miller, Ann Ward, Jessica Howarth, Drew Nelles, and Gillian Sze.

Thanks also to Elee Kraljii Gardiner, Melissa Thompson, Felicity Tayler, and Alison Winch for support and encouragement.

Heartfelt thanks to my immediate and extended family. Especially to my mother, Suzanne Blouin, my sister, Pascale Rafie, and my niece, Mélina Costa.

ABOUT THE AUTHOR

Melissa Bull is a writer and editor, as well as a French-to-English translator of fiction, essays, and plays. She is the editor of *Maisonneuve* magazine's "Writing from Quebec" column and has published her poetry, essays, articles, and interviews in a variety of publications including *Event, Lemon Hound, subTerrain, Prism International,* and *Matrix.* She is the author of a collection of poetry, *Rue* (2015, Anvil Press), and the translator of Nelly Arcan's *Burqa de chair* (*Burqa of Skin,* 2014, Anvil Press), and Marie-Sissi Labrèche's *Borderline* (2019, Anvil Press). Melissa lives in Montreal.